CW01623252

The Last Carol at Christmas

By Frankie Franklin

Stave I

1853 London
Christmas Eve

Stave II

The Ghost of Christmas Past?

Stave III

The Ghost of Christmas Presents

Stave IV

The Ghost of Christmas Yet to Come

Stave V

The Last Carol at Christmas

Stave I

1853 London

To begin with, Marley was still dead, there is no doubt about that.

It will be seventeen years this very night since he passed.

Old Marley is still dead, dead as a doornail.

This must be distinctly understood, or nothing wonderful can come from this story I am going to relate.

Christmas Eve

The sign outside of the counting house looks freshly painted and has at least two inches of fresh snow upon its top edge, the dark green background is shadowed by the greyness of the day but the bright yellow lettering shines as a rare glimpse of winter sun strikes across it for just a second. It declares 'Scrooge and Marley', as it has done for many years even after the death of Jacob Marley, Ebenezer Scrooge has kept the company name as it always has been.

The inside of the old counting house is bright with many lit candles placed on cold window ledges, upon the old harsh wooden desks with hinged lids and across the top mantle of every fireplace inside, every fire is lit, there are four in total. Each has a well shined brass scuttle filled to the brim with coals as black as the devils soul and beside each stands sturdy iron companion sets each comprising of a poker, a small shovel, tongs and a rough brush. The door from the counting house to the tiny miserable cell where Bob Cratchit had been apprenticed and then employed as a clerk to Mr. Scrooge and Mr. Marley has been removed, the days of Scrooge spying on his clerk through the just opened door are long gone. Ebenezer Scrooge still works from the counting house and sits at the same desk he always has, Bob Cratchit, his senior clerk for the business shares this workspace with him. Bob has the pleasure of sitting and working from the desk once used by Jacob Marley, a desk that sat idle and cold for many years.

Tim, Tiny Tim as he was known as a boy, has been apprenticed to Scrooge and Marley for nearly a year and works in his father's old workspace. The once cold, dank and tiny area is now warm and welcoming, Tim sits at the very desk that his father had used for many years, he has a new chair with a comfortable cushion seat purchased for him by Scrooge the day he began working, his walking cane with its shaped and curved top hangs on the back of the chair for whenever it needs to be used.

The whole of the counting house is as warm as a freshly toasted slice of thick white bread awaiting the addition of butter and jam to make it complete, the aroma of spices from a warming cauldron of punch fills the air giving the ancient drabness in the room a feeling of Christmas despite there not being a single decoration made of paper, shiny metal foil or popcorn garlands about the place.

The city clocks strike three almost simultaneously as the greyness of the afternoon begins to turn to darkness, it is cold outside with a bleak, biting wind and a hint of fog forms in the air willing itself to take over every nook, cranny and keyhole in the city. Snow is falling as it has been all day, adding to the thick layer of settled snow on the pavements and upon the cobbled street.

"Do not let it boil over man!" Scrooge sounds irritable and cross.

"I won't Sir, see I am stirring it gently to prevent such an occurrence" Bob Cratchit replies as he slowly stirs the warming liquid in the small cauldron hanging over the fire in the main office.

Scrooge scowls and rubs his chin.

"Mmmm, we shall see Mr. Cratchit"

"Don't be such a grouch Uncle Scrooge!" Tim speaks from his small desk in the far corner of the counting house, the same offices that Scrooge and Marley moved into many years ago at Newman's Court near to Cornhill in the City of London.

"Tim!" Bob Cratchit speaks harshly to his son. "In this office please address Mr. Scrooge as Mr. Scrooge and not Uncle Scrooge!"

"Not to fret Bob! Tim is becoming a fine apprentice clerk for our business and he knows when we have clients or tenants in I am Mr. Scrooge and when we don't I am good old Uncle Scrooge!"

"If you say so Sir" Bob replies grumpily.

"Keep stirring man, that is Smoking Bishop in that cauldron, we don't want the sugars, peel and expensive spices to burn do we!" Ebenezer Scrooge winks at Tim who smiles and puts his quill back into the inkwell. "Tim, come along! Get that poker in the fire, it needs to be red hot, hotter than the fires of hell to make the punch taste good!"

Tim gets up from his wooden chair with some difficulty, he reaches for his walking stick and limps across the room to the fire and places the iron poker in the glowing red coals.

"Won't be but a few minutes to get it glowing Uncle Scrooge" Tim says as Bob scowls again but remains silent. "Shall we discuss my Christmas salary rise?" Tim asks playfully.

"No!" Bob stops stirring the cauldron of punch hanging above the fireplace in the part of the office he shares with Mr. Scrooge.

"Fifteen shillings a week is what your Father used to earn as a qualified clerk so fifteen shillings is what you will receive as an apprentice clerk to Scrooge and Marley!" Scrooge replies with a playful cackle to his tone.

The bell on the door jingles merrily and the three men look up as Emily Cratchit arrives, she closes the door quickly as snow blows in and she brushes rapidly melting white flakes from her bonnet.

"Merry Christmas you old miser!" she says to Scrooge. "Not a hint of decoration to celebrate the season, as is usual in here!"

The shock on Bob's face is clear for them all to see, Scrooge steps away from his desk and greets her.

"Always keen to remind me of the old ways Emily!" The old man laughs as the pair hug and she kisses him gently on the cheek.

"This is an office my love, a counting house, a place of work, no decoration is needed" Bob says to her. "Festivities will begin this evening as they always have"

Emily turns her attention back to Scrooge.

"Three sharp tomorrow Ebenezer if you please, Christmas dinner will not wait for you!"

"My love, it is Mr. Scrooge in the office you know that" Bob speaks to his wife firmly.

Scrooge and Emily look at him in silence before they both burst out laughing at Bobs attempt to be the serious man he usually portrays is in the office.

"Humbug Mr. Cratchit!" Scrooge says with joy in his voice. "Will you stay for a glass of festive punch my dear?"

"I thank you but no. I have to be on my way to buy a few last minute surprises" she checks all her buttons on her coat are done up tightly and she tightens the scarf around her neck.

"Surprises?" Bob asks as he stops stirring the punch. "What surprises?"

Scrooge clicks his bony fingers at his senior clerk who immediately resumes stirring the punch slowly.

"They won't be surprises will they if I tell you Robert Cratchit!" she puts her hand onto the doorknob but does not turn it to open the door. "Do not overdo the punch gentlemen, especially you Tim!"

"Yes Mother"

"I am visiting to remind you both, Robert and Tim Cratchit, that as well as final surprises I am also visiting the poulterers to pay for the Christmas goose and you need to collect it for preparation on your way home before it goes to the bakers to be roasted for tomorrow" she looks sternly at both of them. "Or we will be having bread and dripping for our dinner tomorrow!"

"Her Majesty the Queen is having turkey according to our Belinda's husband" Bob tells Mr. Scrooge.

Emily sighs with theatrical drama.

"I prefer goose and so do you Robert, just because Arthur works at the palace does not mean we have to live a Queens life!"

"Emily my dear, let me pay for the Christmas goose" Scrooge steps forward and takes a very old leather purse from his jacket pocket, the leather string around its top is thin and worn. Emily puts her hand over the top of the purse on onto the old man's bent fingers.

"No Ebenezer" she says quietly. "You have done more than enough for us over the years, there is no need for you to pay for your own Christmas dinner"

Scrooge smiles and cragginess of his face is extenuated by the movement of every wrinkle on his old cheeks.

"But for many years I made Bob's life very unpleasant and inadvertently, without care or thought, your family suffered because of my actions. I have need to make amends the mistakes of my past" he looks at the three members of the Cratchit family with gratitude for their friendship, he grins showing several gaps in his teeth. "It was turkey that first year, I sent it secretly by cab from the poulterers at Leadenhall Market, do you recall?"

"I do recall Ebenezer, as well you know! It was as big as Tiny Tim was and I also recall that it was a secret you kept for several Christmases!" she kisses him gently on the cheek for the second time. "You have done more than enough for us, for others and most importantly for yourself. You know the agreement, one year you come to us for Christmas dinner, the next you visit your nephew and his wife, then on the third year we all come to your house and poor Mrs. Dilber cooks for all of us!"

The door to the counting house bursts open and Emily has to jump backward to avoid being clattered by it. Fred, Scrooges nephew bursts in and as is usual for him at this time of year, he is aglow with a face as ruddy and handsome as it has always been.

"A merry Christmas Uncle, God save you!" he bellows as snow and fog filter into the room behind him, it is then he notices that Emily has stepped back from his dramatic entrance almost in fright. "My dear Mrs. Cratchit, I hope my arrival in this manner has not taken away your breath or damaged your beautiful fragility?" he steps forward and kisses her on the hand. "Such loveliness should never be scared and breathless with fright at Christmas!"

He closes the door leaving the snow, cold and fog of winter outside.

"Fred Hollywell you are a dreadful human being!" she smiles as he kisses her hand for a second time. "Please remember me to Lily and wish her a wonderful Christmas" Emily looks directly at him. "Even if she has to spent it with you"

"And the children, don't forget the children!" Scrooge laughs raucously as they talk.

"Of course, our regards to Samuel, Noah and Frances" Emily says. "Are they all excited about Christmas day?" she asks.

"Samuel is nine now and has clearly stated that he saw Father Christmas last year and recognised his green robes, red hat, red breeches with the shiniest black boots, not forgetting his huge white beard. Samuel is certain to speak to him on this Christmas!" he laughs again. "Noah who was six just last week" he turns to Scrooge. "We thank you for his gift Uncle, as usual you have been very generous to our children" Scrooge nods silently as Fred continues. "And Frances, Fan to Uncle Scrooge of course, is three years old and she is as bright as a button every second of everyday and very excited about tomorrow, she told Lily just this morning that she will not be able to sleep a wink tonight with excitement"

"Dear Fan, she reminds me so much of your mother Fred" Scrooge says with hints of sadness in his voice. "I miss my little sister every day"

"Fear not Uncle, although you dine with the Cratchits this year, the Holywell's will raise a glass to you and to my dearly departed Mother, your beloved sister" Fred turns to speak to Bob and Tim. "I did not really know my father, he was James Holywell and served in the army and was killed in 1836 in Spain whilst serving with the Westminster Legion, I was at boarding school at the time. As you know my mother gave her life for me as I was born"

Scrooge wipes a tear from his eye.

"And I blamed you for many years for that Fred, I am sorry and I am sure you know it now"

"I do Uncle and I am happy we have been acquainted properly this past decade!" he waves his arms around at every corner of the office. "How this has changed from a dismal place of lending money with extortionate fees and interest, it now helps those who need it, the poor and the destitute with charitable donations, you help others manage their own funds and to live as well as they can"

Scrooge is embarrassed and is glad to hear carol singing start outside of the door of the counting house.

"O Come all ye faithful, joyful and triumphant..."

Scrooge throws open the door and faces the group of children singing outside of his office.

"O come ye, o come ye to Bethlehem..." the children continue singing as Scrooge stares at them.

"O come and behold him, born the King of Angels..." the sound of the young voices is stunning in the cold night air. Scrooge joins in.

"O come, let us adore him, O come let us adore him" he turns to the three other men in the office and waves his hands at them, they also join in to finish the chorus.

"O come let us adore him, Christ the lord!" the children cheer with happiness and Scrooge takes out his leather purse and hands over coins to the child at the front.

"To be shared equally" he says as he rubs the boys hair, he turns to Fred who steps forward and hands over coins from his pocket. Scrooge looks at Bob who has not moved, he coughs with more drama than is necessary and nods at the children"

"I am still stirring Sir, you said I had to keep on stirring" Bob replies.

"Pish and tish man! A few seconds to give these singing angels a shilling or two will not harm the punch" Scrooge scolds his senior clerk.

"Here, give it to me husband, I will stir whilst you empty your pockets for the carol singers"

"Yes Sir, yes Emily" Bob smiles and leaves the ladle in the punch for his wife to retrieve, he hands over a few coins to the children"

"Thank you Mr. Scrooge!" the children all shout in unison.

"You are welcome, Merry Christmas to all!" Scrooge replies as the children move off the nearby shops and offices hoping to gain a few more shillings and pennies for their singing.

Scrooge closes the door quietly and Bob returns to stirring the punch.

"You have always been a decent man Fred, far more decent that I ever was. Merry Christmas"

Fred puts his hand upon his chin as if trying to remember something important, a huge smile breaks out across his face.

"What else can I be?" says Scrooge's nephew. "When I live in such a world of fools as this. Merry Christmas! Out upon merry Christmas. What is Christmas time to you but a time for paying bills without money, a time for finding yourself a year older, but not an hour richer, a time for balancing your books and having every item in 'em thought a round dozen of months presented dead against you? If I could work my will, every idiot who goes around with 'Merry Christmas' on his lips, should be boiled with his own pudding, and buried with a stake of holly through his heart. He should!"

Bob giggles as Emily and Tim look at each other with confused looks on their faces.

"You are still quite the powerful speaker sir, your memory for my words is encouraging nephew, there is hope for you yet!" Scrooge says with a lilt of happiness in his tone. "I am glad with all my heart that you are not so resolute as I was, I am glad we have never had any quarrel to which I have been party and I hope I have made this trial in homage to Christmas and I hope to keep Christmas humour to my last. So, a very Merry Christmas to you Nephew!"

The old man and Fred shake hands as Bob claps in the background.

"I am rich in my heart Uncle"

"As am I nephew and I thank you for that"

"Keep stirring that punch husband or the miser and his obviously deranged nephew will berate you for burning it!"

"Dear lady, I apologise for any confusion, words spoken many years ago still have meaning, especially at this time of year" Fred opens the door and stands to attention as the cold air breaks into the warmth of the room.

"Merry Christmas Fred Holywell" she turns to her husband and son. "Don't forget the goose, be warned!"

"Until tomorrow then!" Scrooge calls at Emily who is walking away from the counting house and disappears into the fog and snow, he closes the door gently. "Poker young Tim, poker!"

Fred rubs his hands together with glee as Tim takes the glowing poker from the fire in his part of the office and walks it ceremoniously into the main counting house with the aid of his stick. Fred has taken four clear glass bowls from the shelf by Scrooges desk and they stand around the steaming cauldron with its steaming liquid still being agitated by Bob.

"Stop stirring man!" Scrooge demands as he ushers Tim forward, avoiding any contact with the red hot iron poker. "Now!" Scrooge, with childlike gusto encourages Tim to step forward.

The poker is plunged into the punch and it immediately bubbles and pulses as though alive, the room is filled with sweet and spicy steam, the poker is removed and Bob ladles generous amounts of the festive punch into each bowl. The four men stand with both hands cupped around the bowls, they sip gently and in silence for a minute or so.

"Merry Christmas Bob Cratchit" Fred speaks first.

"And to you Sir" Bob replies.

Tim is not speaking as he is slurping the delicious warm punch very quickly.

"Slowly Tim!" scolds his father with gentle humour.

"Your Mother would be so proud of you Fred" Scrooge says quietly.

"And of you Uncle" Fred puts his hand onto Scrooges shoulder.

"God bless us, everyone" Tim says as he finishes his bowl.

Tim and Bob are clearing the office and filing the final documents of the day, Fred prepares to leave after his second bowl of punch, he wishes the Cratchits all the best for a fabulous Christmas day and ensures that his Uncle Scrooge will arrive in time for lunch with him and Lily on the second day of Christmastide.

"The Feast of Stephen will be gargantuan Uncle!" he proclaims. "Then, as you have requested we will visit some of your tenants in Camden Town with some parcels of food and drink for their families, then perhaps a brisk walk through Regents Park"

"I thank you Fred, I am so glad I took over the terraces at Bayham Street, it holds a strong memory for me"

Fred then took his leave and is heard singing Silent Night as he walks toward Cornhill.

"Mrs. Cratchit and I really liked living at number sixteen Bayham Street, such happy times when the children were young!' Bob is happy as he replies and thinks of the memory.

"Indeed Mr. Cratchit but I certainly recall that the four room house was quite tight with the six of you cramped in there"

Bob nods slowly.

"I agree Sir and the home we have now, thanks to you, seems substantially larger now that it is only Emily, Tim and I living there"

Scrooge chuckles.

"It will be full to briming tomorrow Bob when they all come back for the day.

"You are welcome to come for a meal this evening Sir" Bob adds.

"No thank you Bob, I will be happy in my rooms at my end of Lime Street"

"Have you ever considered moving away Uncle Scrooge, I mean your home is huge but it is quite a gloomy suite of rooms that you really do not need. I feel sorry for Mrs. Dilber, cleaning all those rooms that you never use!"

"You never complained as a lad when you were charging around the place, up and down the stairs making a racket enough to waken the dead!"

"And did it?" Tim laughs as he asks the question.

"Of course not" Scrooge replies quietly, then whispers to himself. "Some of the dead never get the chance to sleep"

"Did you say something Sir?" Bob asks as he stands next to his desk. "We are just about done here for the day if you please."

Scrooge looks up with a scowl on his face.

"You'll want all day tomorrow, I suppose?" Scrooge asks them both.

"If it is quite convenient Sir" Bob answers with a huge smile on his face.

"I think it is! I am spending the day with my senior clerk and his family and I am very much looking forward to it" Scrooge puts his hand on Bob's shoulder. "I really am looking forward to it all my friend"

"You will be very welcome Sir" Bob tells him.

"If you are at Fred's on the Feast of St Stephen, does that mean Father and I can have the day as well?" Tim calls from his desk, he adds. "Mr. Scrooge if you please!"

"Another days wages for no work Mr. Cratchit?" Scrooge asks Bob.

"I know it's a poor excuse for picking a man's pocket every twenty fifth of December.."

"And the twenty sixth" Scrooge butts in. "But I suppose if you must have the whole of Christmas day you may as well have the following day"

"If any man alive possesses the knowledge of how to keep Christmas well it is you Sir, you are a good master, a good man and a good friend"

"Get off with you Mr. Cratchit and take Master Cratchit with you!"

"Until tomorrow Uncle Scrooge!" Tim says before adding "We have finished for the day now Father!" when he sees Bob looking at him sternly once again.

"Merry Christmas to all the Cratchits!" Scrooge pats them both on the back as they leave for the short journey to their home.

"Don't work late Sir"

"I won't Bob, have a splendid evening and I will see you for lunch tomorrow, don't forget to collect the goose, if it is not prepared and at the bakers oven we shall all starve without doubt!"

"Thank you Sir, please don't be late for Christmas lunch, you know what a stickler Emily is!"

"You are a very lucky man Bob Cratchit"

Scrooge closes the door then nips out all the candles in area Tim works in, he pokes the fires to help them to begin to die down. The city clocks strike five, Scrooge looks at his pocket watch and sits at his desk, he takes two old pennies from the pocket in his jacket, he rubs them gently before putting them back, these are the pennies he took from the eyes of Jacob Marley as he lay dead on Christmas Eve 1836. He has carried them with him ever since, oddly they give him comfort.

"You are late Mr. Granger" Scrooge tells his visitor.

"Just a few minutes Mr. Scrooge, my apologies" he accepts a bowl of punch from Scrooge. "I thank you Sir, this is warming and welcome, the conditions outside are worsening by the hour it feels"

Scrooge looks through the window of the counting house and sees people rushing home with the rising wind blowing the snow around in dervishes of white turbulence, the fog seems worse than it was when Bob and Tim left just fifteen or so minutes ago.

"The fire in here still glows should you wish to move closer to it Mr. Granger. I would be obliged if we could move on with our business as I wish to get to my home and warm my chamber through before supper"

"As you wish Mr. Scrooge"

Mr. Granger opens his leather satchel and removes a single document written in neat old English script, the header of the document is written in letters twice the size of the remainder of the words upon it.

This is the Last Will and Testament

of

Ebenezer Scrooge

"The document is legally binding from this very evening, as soon as we have both signed it in fact and it will make any other written wills null and void"

"I understand Sir, have the changes been made as requested?" Scrooge asks the lawyer who nods several times.

"Indeed, your previous will from..." he looks at other documents he has taken from the satchel. "January first, 1844." he pauses without reason before speaking again. "To confirm the will and its changes with you Mr. Scrooge. Firstly, and without change, a sum of five thousand pounds and all properties owned by Scrooge and Marley at Bayham Street, Camden Town, to be bequeathed to Mr. Frederick Holywell of number one Leadenhall Street, London, bar number sixteen" he looks up at Scrooge. "This marks the first change from the former document, that single property is now to pass to one Mr. Timothy Cratchit" he looks at Scrooge. "You are changing this property in your will from Mr. Robert Cratchit to Mr. Timothy Cratchit, is that correct?"

"It is Sir"

Granger finishes his bowl of punch, thanking his host he then continues.

"The business of Scrooge and Marley is to be left in its entirety, to include all buildings and properties owned by it and all monies left after you have passed, I have to stress this does include any debt owed by your good self or the business"

"There is no debt, never has been and I am sure there never will be Sir!. The financial ledgers are accurate to the last penny with all taxes paid, charitable donations are to continue from the business of course"

"Indeed Mr. Scrooge, that caveat is included as it has been since 1844. To confirm the business and everything it owns is to be left to Mr. Robert Cratchit of number two Lime Street, London"

"Correct" Scrooge has a smile as he speaks.

"Mr. Cratchit will be able to pay off any loans and mortgages on that property after you pass Sir, a very generous bequeath"

"There is no mortgage or loans on the property Sir. Cratchit thinks I own it but all the documents that sit with your company are in his name, I presume I need not bequeath this as it is owned by him although he does not know it?"

Granger is taken aback.

"A generous gift Mr. Scrooge, it is my presumption that you lodged that particular document with my Father?"

"I did Sir, a good man, he also wrote and prepared the original will for me in 1844"

"Sorely missed by us all Mr. Scrooge" the lawyer looks sad for a second or two. "Shall I continue?"

"Please" Scrooge is feeling tired and wants this legal process to be over.

"A change in your final property Mr. Scrooge, you now require your home at 45 Lime Street, London to be sold by Scrooge and Marley and the proceeds from it to be equally split between four London charities. The Poor Man's Guardian Society, The Orphan's Working School, the Royal Hospital for the Incurable and finally the Hospital for Sick Children. This property is no longer to form part of those owned by this company, therefore Mr. Cratchit will not inherit 45 Lime Street"

"Correct Sir, the hospital treated my apprentice clerk when he was a boy, a fine hospital deserving of a gift"

Granger nods happily.

"Your share of the feast of love and kindness is both generous and charitable Sir, your charitable soul has and will continue to contribute to the happiness of the world"

"I thank you for your words Mr. Granger, you should meet my nephew Fred, he is also quite the powerful speaker, I once suggested he take up in Parliament"

"Oh my, most certainly not for me I can assure you!" Granger adjusts the spectacles on his face. "And finally Mr. Scrooge, your housekeeper Mrs. Louisa Dilber is to be bequeathed an annual sum of twenty pounds to be paid from the business of Scrooge and Marley on each twenty fourth of December"

"Mrs. Dilber has worked for me for many a year and I have not, I am unhappy to say, always been the easiest of men to get along with"

"A tidy sum for a housekeeper Sir, twenty pounds is, I would suggest, almost double what the lady earns now"

Scrooge is feeling so very tired and feelings if irritability rise in his very soul, he fights and subdues them successfully.

"It matters not what the lady earns Mr. Granger, the sum is to be paid annually to her until her death"

"Very good Mr. Scrooge. If you would care to read through the document then we can sign and it will be legally binding, even should you die seconds after it will be bound by law"

Scrooge smiles and touches his chest with his right fist.

"I have no intention of dying today or for some time Mr. Granger" he then taps the document. "I am feeling tired Sir, can I have your word that the changes have been made and documented correctly as stated?"

"You have it Sir" Mr. Granger replies solemnly.

"Then I shall sign without delay"

Scrooge dabs his quill into the ink pot on his desk and signs his name without flair or exaggeration on the document.

The witness line is signed using the same quill by Mr. Joshua Andrew Granger esq. Lawyer.

"All done Mr. Scrooge"

"I thank you Sir for stepping out on this most awful of evenings. Will you be rushing home to your family for Christmas now?"

"I will Sir, firstly I will stop in at my business chambers and file this very important document away in a safe place"

"As my legal representative you will be advised of my passing when the time comes?"

"We will Sir, I will then ensure that your Last Will and Testament is executed to the very letter you have instructed. Shall I bill Scrooge and Marley for this most recent transaction?"

"No" Scrooge takes out his purse yet again. "I will complete the transaction now if it pleases"

"That will be most decent of you Mr. Scrooge. As agreed the preparation and writing of the will and the continued storage will be costed at one guinea"

"Still using old money even though it has not been in circulation for nearly 4 decades!" Scrooge giggles quietly.

"Lawyers and racehorse owners still deal in the guinea Sir"

Scrooge counts out twenty one shillings.

"Legal extortion Mr. Granger!"

The lawyer is about to retort when he sees the playful glint in Scrooges eyes.

"Indeed Mr. Scrooge, indeed it is" they both chuckle. "Will you take your evening meal at the Tavern Sir?"

Scrooge takes out his pocket watch and looks at the time.

"No Sir, no melancholy meal in the melancholy Simpsons tavern for me this evening. I have a full day tomorrow celebrating Christmas day with friends, I am mightily looking forward to it. So a quiet bowl of soup in my chamber and then I'll retire to bedlam Sir, to prepare for the festivities"

The documents are folded neatly and placed back into an envelope of fine quality, Granger takes a small wooden item from his pocket, he points at the candle alight on the desk.

"May I Sir?" he asks Scrooge who nods without answering. Mr. Granger lifts the candle over the back of the envelope and pours hot wax onto it, he takes the small wooden tool and pushes it into the quickly drying wax. "All sealed and it will remain so until it need be broken" the envelope is put gently into his satchel.

"Merry Christmas to you Mr. Scrooge"

The lawyer and the businessman shake hands.

"And to you Mr. Granger"

As Scrooge locks up his place of business 'God rest ye merry gentlemen' is being sung by a group of heavily wrapped up carol singers, scarves, hats and gloves are being warn by each and every one of them. The lanterns they carry glow dimly through the fog and snow, Scrooge lifts his hat a few inches from his head, wishes them a very merry Christmas and places a generous donation into the charity tin being carried by the smallest child in the group.

The courtyard at 45 Lime Street is dark and heavy with fog, snow and frost at its gateway, even Scrooge who knows every nook of this yard has to feel his way along the familiar stones to get to the substantial front door of the property as no gas lamps are lit in the street here. His mind flashes back to another Christmas eve when the weather was as it is this very night, a night he thinks about often, a night he has never uttered a single word about to another living soul since it happened, a night that was at first filled with fear that chilled his blood.

Christmas Eve 1843.

Taking his brass headed stick he raises it as he stares intently at the door knocker that had once taken the form of Jacob Marley, he recalls the dismal light about it, not angry or ferocious but as Marley had looked in life. Spectacles turned up on his forehead with whisps of ethereal hair stirred up by breath or hot air, his eyes were wide open but motionless, his look was one of fear and horror, a look that Ebenezer Scrooge clearly remembered to this very moment.

"Jacob Marley!" Scrooge speaks aloud as he looks around the dark courtyard, he raps the doorknocker with the head of his stick. "Jacob Marley!" he said once more.

The lack of any answer or vision pleased Scrooge, he laughs out loud in the dark as he takes out the huge old key and turns it into the lock, twists the brass door knob and pushes open the door. Unlike that night ten years previously when the house had been cold and dark, he feels warmth flowing from inside and it relaxes the chilled skin upon his face.

"Mrs. Dilber, you are a saint" Scrooge says aloud as he closes the door and lights the candle that always sits on the small table by the door. "Coming home to a warm house with a lit fire warms the soul" he takes off his jacket and hangs it on the stand in the hallway.

The clock on the church next door strikes six times with the pause between each strike exactly as the pause before it. The door is locked and the knocker that once held a vision of Scrooges dead partner is left alone facing the dark courtyard.

The soup is pea and ham and it is delicious, Mrs. Dilber had obviously made it earlier for him and all Ebenezer had to do was to warm it through on the fire, a fire that needed little attention to bring it back to full life. As his soup was warming through he had changed from his work attire and was comfortably dressed in a nightshirt, slippers and a heavy dressing gown, his nightcap lies upon the pillow of the substantial bed that dominates the room, its curtains pulled back and no longer used by the old man. The only light in the room is from the glow of the fire, Scrooge had extinguished the candle as he sat down for his supper, he no longer cared that darkness was cheap as he once had, he finds it comforting as it envelopes him and he feels protected by its unseeing grip.

The fireplace is as unchanged as the rest of the building, built by a Dutch merchant so long ago and paved around with tiles designed to illustrate scriptures, Cains and Abel's mixed with the daughters of Pharaohs and Queens of Sheba, Angels descending upward on clouds alongside Abraham, Belshazzar and Apostles at sea in butter boats, the hundreds of figures keep Scrooge occupied as the surround had on many occasions previously. As he had done some ten years previously he stares intently at each tile looking for a copy of Marley's head on every on and as it had been in 1843, he does not see a single tile with his seventeen year dead partners face upon it.

"Humbug!" Scrooge says aloud to himself with more than a little humour and satisfaction in his voice.

"Humbug Ebenezer? Surely not!"

Scrooge is startled and throws his bowl of soup, it hits the tiles surrounding the fireplace and breaks into several pieces with the thick pea and ham liquid dripping down, firstly covering the Queen of Sheba before commencing its journey toward the hearth via Abraham, Cain, Abel and all the others.

He knows the voice instantly.

"Jacob Marley?" he said with alarming calmness. "You visit me yet again?"

"Turn to face me Ebenezer Scrooge, turn to admire the changes in me, changes you have made to me!"

Scrooge turns his head but remains seated in his chair facing the roaring fire.

The ghost of Jacob Marley stands in the middle of his chamber, the face, the very same face he had last seen ten years ago this very evening, he is dressed as he was then, pigtail coat, usual waistcoat, tights and boots, everything about him is as transparent as it was. The folded kerchief still bound about his head and chin as he had observed on the ghosts previous visit.

"Your clothes are outdated Jacob!" Scrooge says to the ghost. "Can you still sit?"

"I can" Marley does not move. "Do you see no differences to me Ebenezer?" he asks.

"You are as dead as you were seventeen years ago this night are you not?"

"I am" Marley chuckled, it is a sound that Scrooge had never heard during the life of Jacob Marley or when he had appeared as a phantom ten years ago, the sound is muffled due to the restriction of the kerchief. "Do you believe in me?" the ghost asks.

Ebenezer found himself smiling as Marley made his way across the room, almost floating and into the armchair on the opposite side of the fireplace, the very same chair he had sat in previously.

"I do believe in you Jacob, not as an undigested piece of beef, a blot of mustard or a crumb of cheese or an underdone potato but as Jacob Marley, unsettled, condemned and doomed to wander through this world of the living after death, fettered by the chains, boxes, ledgers and padlocks you forged in life" he stares wide eyed at the ghost sitting opposite him. "Jacob you are unfettered, I see not a single chain or wrought iron box, no padlocks or cash boxes, you are free!"

"I asked if you could see a difference in me and you have seen it" Marley speaks quietly to Scrooge. "This difference is because of the changes in you Ebenezer Scrooge and this is my last night on mortal earth as a spirit, now I am free from restrictions, free from the unyielding pain of walking amongst the living without rest, I am free to move on"

"To where Jacob, move on to where?" Scrooge leans forward in his chair so as to hear Marley clearly.

"To rest Ebenezer, seventeen years without rest as a ghost is tiresome, seventeen years burdened by the weight of my actions on earth, but this has been lifted. Since you have become a different man, since you moved on, every year my weights and chains became less until they were no more"

"I am pleased for you Jacob" Scrooge stares into the flames as he speaks again. "When did the last weight lift your soul free?"

Marley looks at Scrooge with undead staring eyes.

"Today, this very day the final link of chain fell away and I felt the lifting of every wrongdoing and every business completed that harmed another. I am free Ebenezer Scrooge and tonight I move into a spirit life that I can only hope will be brighter and lighter than the one I have lived since death"

Scrooge wrings his bony hands and seems concerned and distracted.

"I am pleased for you Jacob, I will look to see you no more after this night"

"What worries you Scrooge, what perturbs you?" Marley asks as Ebenezer looks directly into the unseeing eyes of his dead partner. "Is it your weight, the length of the strong coil that I warned you were as heavy and as long as mine some seventeen years ago?"

"It is" Scrooge replies in a barely audible whisper.

"Mankind has become your business, common welfare has become your business, charity, forbearance and benevolence have all become your business. The final link in your chain died this day, the disappearance of the final link in your chain removed the final link in mine"

"I am satisfied I was able to set you free old friend, glad your penance is finally over"

"As am I, my penance is complete, at an end" Marley moves his head stiffly to look in the direction of Scrooge. "As is your time on this earth"

Ebenezer jumps up from his chair, a look of fear across his face, the same look that Marley had seen ten years previous.

"No Jacob, say it is not so! I said it before to you and I will ask it again, speak comfort to me"

"These are words of comfort, this is the end of your life, your last days"

Scrooge is scared and it shows as he begins to pace around the chamber, in and out of the shadows. Marley does not move.

"Speak to me Jacob! Tell me when and why?"

"I cannot. I cannot because I am not informed as to when or why, but see it as a gift Ebenezer. How many men know when their life is over? Knowing they can lie in their bed with peace in their heart and without pain?"

Scrooge continues to pace around the room, talking as he moves.

"I have so much more to give Jacob, I am not ready to die"

Marley chuckles again and Ebenezer finds it as disconcerting as he did earlier.

"No one is ready to die Mr. Scrooge! No one can really be prepared for it! But you can try to be prepared, this is a gift to you, a chance to leave this life with calm in your soul"

"I have so much more to give" Scrooge repeats his words from moments ago. "I want the workhouses and the prisons to be freed of those wretches who do not deserve to be there, whose only crime is being poor and who still get sent by law or go of their own free will because the life they have is so bad that a better option is to go into institutions run by barbarians!"

"You have worked hard to help those who needed it, but not everyone can be reached, the future is as it is. There are still prisons?" Marley asks with more than a hint of sarcasm in his tone.

"Plenty of prisons" Scrooge replies seemingly ignoring the sarcastic words. He retakes his seat, he feels calmer though not accepting of his position.

"And the union workhouses?" asks Marley. "Still all in operation?"

"They are Jacob, the treadmill and the Poor Law are still in full vigour" Marley remains silent as Scrooge stares into the flickering flames of the fire. "I wish I could say that they were not"

"Both very busy?" Marley speaks without emotion.

"Yes they are, this is why this cannot be my last days of life, I still have much to do!"

Marley stands up and points to the window and to the darkness beyond.

"The air outside is still filled with phantoms, those who had no help in their life, they wander hither and thither in permanent restless haste"

Scrooge stands up and walks to the window, all he can see is the darkness of the evening outside.

"I do not see them this time Jacob, surely my good works have saved some souls from this torment?"

Marley instructs Scrooge to open the sash window, the old man does as he is told.

"Look carefully Ebenezer"

Scrooge places both palms of his hands on the outside sill, he feels the coldness of the snow pierce his skin like tiny needles, he squints his eyes and he sees them.

Phantoms, ghosts, spirits move silently through the still darkness of the London evening, the living do not see them and carry on with their busy lives without interaction or cause to be involved.

"So many" he whispers.

He then begins to hear the screams of those tormented to walk the earth in the afterlife, whether constricted by chains or by situation they are there in their hundreds, possibly thousands. The screams become louder and louder and Scrooge places his cold hands over his ears in an attempt to stop the noise.

"Jacob have mercy! Make it stop!" Scrooge has to shout loudly to be heard over the screams and cries coming from the ethereal beings on the outside.

Marley stands up and claps his transparent hands together, as he does the window slams shut and the noise abates instantly, Scrooge takes his hands away from his ears slowly until he is satisfied the horrible sounds have stopped.

"You will be visited again by three ghosts" Jacob tells him.

"Haunted? Again? Why Jacob, why?"

"You were a good friend to me in life Ebenezer and a better one in death and I thank you for that"

"Why will I need to see the same three ghosts on these my last nights on earth?" he pleads to the ghost that has moved toward the closed door of the chamber. "I have worked so hard to be given a second chance have I not?"

"You have Ebenezer and this could be it" Marley faces his friend for the last time.

"I don't understand, the chains and shackles are gone, you told me so, those hardships for others I forged in life have been removed. Am I not to be forgiven?"

"It was never about forgiveness friend, it has always been about amending wrongs we committed. You have done enough to remove not only your chains but mine as well. I thank you for this, I thank you for giving my life back in death"

"Thanks is not needed." Scrooge rubs his eyes to stop tears falling. "What do I do now Jacob?"

"Take those coins from your jacket, the very coins that were on my eyes on the night I passed, take them and place them one on top of the other on your bedside stand"

"Why?" Scrooge sounds confused. "Why do I need to do this?"

Jacob Marley moves through the closed door and disappears.

"Jacob?" Scrooge calls out.

"Look to see me no more Ebenezer Scrooge" a voice in the darkness fades as it speaks.

Scrooge is alone in the near darkness of the room, the fire is dying and needs fuel adding or to be poked.

Scrooge does neither.

Stave II
Ghost of Christmas past?

Scrooge stands alone in the near darkness of the room, he hears the church clock strike seven, only an hour since he arrived home from the office and it seems a lifetime has passed in his mind. He sees that the fire is dying and needs fuel adding to it or to be poked to bring it back to life. He does neither, he stands as still as a statue and as silent as a hibernating mouse in the ever darkening room.

Suddenly the room is filled with light, a light so bright that Ebenezer has to cup his hands over his eyes, a memory stirs in his mind, a memory of a light as bright as this from many years previous.

"Spirit is that you?" he calls out through the brightness. "We met before, a Christmas past?"

"You asked me to dim my light, to dim my life, you begged me to be covered. Should I do so again?"

"Only so I can see you spirit" Scrooge stammered. "I have no desire to dim your life but I am blinded"

The brightness in the room drops considerably, enough for Scrooge to make out the spirit that now shares the space in his chamber with him. It is a familiar sight for the old man, the spirit has changed hardly at all in the decade since the last visit. It's childlike appearance with the grace and features of an old man are unchanged, his appearance is not full and occasionally recedes and diminishes from his view. It has pure white hair that hangs as it did before about his neck and onto his back, yet the old face still has not a single discernible wrinkle upon it. The tunic of purest white is as untouched and as clean as freshly laundered linen with the belt securing the tunic as lustrous and beautiful as he remembered it to be. It remains, with the strangest quality, in that it sparkles and glitters in one part then in an instant in another, seemingly in tune with the occasional diminishment of its fullest figure.

In one hand, the sprig of green holly with blood red berries seems unchanged and the extinguisher cap is still under its other arm but the most memorable thing about the ghost of Christmas past is the bright clear jet of light emanating from the crown of its head.

"You have changed a little I feel spirit" Scrooge says quietly.

"In what way have I changed Ebenezer Scrooge?" the voice from the spirit carries across the room and penetrates the very being of the old man.

"You remain distinct and clear, although moving in and out of my view, you remain whole. If memory serves me well and I believe it does, when we first met your figure fluctuated and changed from having one leg then twenty legs then without a head and a head without a body and when the changes happened there was no outline in the gloom of my chamber wherein you melted away before becoming one again with clearer and distinct lines"

The spirit shimmered but remained whole with a distinctly human form.

"We all change over time, look how you have evolved" the voice of the spirit a whisper that is almost alive in Scrooges ear.

"Are you still the ghost of Christmas past?"

"I am."

"Long past?" Scrooge asked the same question when the spirit visited him previously.

"Your past Ebenezer Scrooge" the answer is also the same.

"Why? Who's past? We have done this all before" Scrooge tells the ghost.

"There is a new past if you choose to have it so, to witness a change in the past if you so wish"

Scrooge is suddenly attentive and steps toward the spirit with his arms in front of him almost pleading.

"Spirit, can you change.."

The spirit becomes translucent and his form wavers in front of Scrooge for a second.

"Ebenezer Scrooge, I am the ghost of Christmas past, I cannot change, alter or stop any decisions that are yet to be made"

"But this could be my last night on...."

The spirit stops him again as it disappears for a long two or three seconds, the brightness in the room remains although the darkness outside threatens to penetrate through the heavily frosted window.

"I cannot change, alter or stop any decisions that are yet to be made, I am the ghost of Christmas past"

"You can change my past?" Scrooge asks.

"If I will it, it can be done" the spirit re appears and its form remains solid, the light emanating from its crown may be the tiniest bit less bright than it was.

"Spirit, are you quite well?"

"A strange question for an age old spirit" Scrooge shrugs, sighs but gives no reply. "You have had a life of fulfilment Ebenezer, you are cleansed and forgiven for all your previous actions, your views and your attitude toward your fellow man"

Scrooge looks at the floor as he replies.

"I did what had to be done but not just for me, I knew I had to change but I wanted so to change the lives of others and I thought I had more to offer"

"You may still have things to offer. I can offer it to you but it is not what you really want at this very moment in time, I cannot change, alter or stop any decisions that are yet to be made"

"I know and I am sad about that and admittedly a little afraid" Scrooge sits in the chair, the fire is almost out but the room is no longer dark and cold, the spirit brings light and warmth with it.

"I can pass on one wish for change, we can re visit what you witnessed the last time we met, you can change one thing and one thing only. The choice must be yours and not influenced by others" the spirit moves around the room creating flashes of shadows in the corners of the chamber as it does so.

"I do not have a choice in whom I ask or consult about this? What changes could I make to change my life as it was?" Scrooge seems confused and is almost talking to himself.

"Things do not have to change but you have one opportunity to do so, you can of course leave the past as it is and it will play out exactly as it has"

Scrooge puts his face into his hands and begins to weep.

"But I hurt so many people, I ignored the pain and harshness in the lives of many"

"You changed Ebenezer, you changed for the good so perhaps we should leave it alone" the spirit moves to be next to the weeping old man.

"But what if I can change things to make things better before I became who I am now? What if I can be a better man from the past? Surely that can only be good for many and be good for humanity?"

"The choice is yours" replies the spirit. "We can re visit your past for a second time and you can choose, or things can be left as they were and stay as they became"

Scrooge stands up and wipes the tears from his face.

"Change for the better spirit, I was unpleasant to many people for many years, a change in the past may just be what is needed, not just for me but for all those I wronged!"

The spirit puts out his arm, the sprig of holly still grasped tightly in his hand.

"As before, bear but a touch of my hand there and you shall be upheld in more than this"

Scrooge moves across the room and takes up his night cap, putting it on his head.

"I will not be cold spirit" he says before reaching out and taking the arm or the ghost of Christmas past.

His words are barely spoken when they pass through the window that opens as they approach and slams shut as they leave, almost immediately they stand on an open country road with vast fields on either side. The darkness of the winter city night has vanished and it is a clear, cold, winter country day with thick snow laying on the hardened ground.

"Here again" Scrooge says quietly, his breath freezing in the air as he speaks.

"You recall this place Ebenezer?" the spirit asks, its breath does not freeze on the icy air.

"I do and I do not wish to revisit it at all, not even if blindfolded!" he becomes cross and upset.

"We can only revisit the places we came to previously" the spirit speaks with calmness and without annoyance at Scrooges ire.

"This place brings only sadness to my memory" Scrooge hangs his head.

"I recall you had almost instant joy when you saw the boys you were at this school with Ebenezer" the spirit moves to be in front of the old man. "You named each and every one as they passed us by"

"I did but they could not see me, they could not see you. I knew them of course but they were not really my friends" he sounds sad and lonely even though he is in the company of the ghost.

"Ali Baba was your friend Ebenezer, books were your friends. We can go back into the school, no one will see us. You must remember what we are seeing are shadows, shadows of the past. Even changes will remain as shadows until the present catches them up, do you still not want to see what the past could have been here Ebenezer?"

"I have nothing to change here spirit, sadness and misery should sometimes be left as it was, a memory to bring current happiness to life, to keep its fires burning. Show me Christmases past here no more!"

"As you wish" the ghost replies.

That moment of the past moves on swiftly, all memories of the school now behind them, a busy thoroughfare of a city has replaced the cold quietness of the countryside.

"Spirit, you told that we would revisit what we saw last time?" Scrooge sounds annoyed.

"I did say that" the ghost replies.

"Then why are we here?" Scrooge is still cross. "This is where I was apprenticed is it not?"

"It is. This is the business warehouse of Mr. Fezziwig, as you recall we visited here to re live your early years as a working man"

"Yes yes, I know that, but you said we would re visit what we saw last time, you have moved too far ahead"

"Have we?" the ghost remains calm despite Scrooges obvious unhappiness at this very moment.

"We have! Indeed we have! After I saw the boys at my school and re lived my loneliness, a place in time I despise, we then moved on to when Fan came to take me away from the school, to rescue my body, my mind and my sanity!"

"Your sister?" Scrooge nods slowly and tears fill his eyes as he recalls her in his mind. "We have moved on at your wish Ebenezer"

"I don't understand. I asked you to show me no more Christmases past at that school, so why are we now in London?" Scrooges anger has been replaced with confusion and sadness emanates from his very soul.

"Where did Fan come to rescue you from Ebenezer? What time of year did she save you from loneliness?" the ghost asks.

Scrooge rubs the night cap on his head and scrunches up his eyes tightly.

"It was Christmas and she came in a carriage to collect me from school, she said that father sent her in a coach to fetch me." the ghost does not move or speak, it only stares at Scrooge. "Spirit, when I said show me no more Christmases at the school I did not mean that time, not then. I only meant the sad times. Fan collecting me and taking me away was a joyous time!"

The ghost waves his arm using the sprig of holly as a pointing stick.

"We are here now Ebenezer, at your request"

"I did not mean it in that way, you must know that!" Scrooge is ready to get on his knees and beg to return, to see his little sister just once more, knowing what the future holds for her is just too much for him to bear.

"We are here now, we must move on as time runs short and decisions have to be made"

Scrooge is forlorn and heartbroken but he also knows the he must move on as the ghost wills, if he has learnt anything at all since he last met this old spook then it is that the past is the past and lessons must be learnt from it.

"We will move on Spirit. I have darkness in my soul at this very moment but we will move on"

"Do you fully understand what is happening and what might be done?" the ghost asks him.

"I think so, the past is the past but I have the opportunity to change one thing from my past"

"Yes, but the visions we are to see are those that the past could have been"

"Not what we saw last time, not what I re lived ten years ago this very night?"

The spirit shakes its head in response, Scrooge falls to his knees and covers his face with his hands.

"If that is what you want to witness then it can be so, but this journey is about re-evaluation, about change if it is deemed to be so"

"I got is so wrong in my mind Spirit!" Scrooge is still on his knees but his arms are now out in front of himself, pleading with the spirit. The hustle and bustle of the busy London street move in and around them both, they remain unseen and the sadness of Scrooge goes unwitnessed.

"I was clear at the start Ebenezer, hear my words"

A vision appears in front of them both, it is a vision of Scrooges chambers and both he and the spirit are present, the spirit speaks.

"There is a new past if you choose to have it so, to witness a change in the past if you so wish"

The vision disappears and Scrooge stands up.

"I missed your words Spirit, I was so caught up in my own demise and wanting that to change that I did not listen clearly"

"This journey is about witnessing change. This journey is about changing the past if it will be of benefit"

"Benefit to whom!" Scrooge points at the spirit as he shouts. "Apologies" he says almost instantly. "This is my mistake and as with all my past mistakes, I shall have to live with them. Please proceed."

"Do you recognise that young man?" the ghost points across the busy street at a man leaving a building, Scrooge smiles.

"I would know that man anywhere, it is Dick Wilkens! We were apprenticed as young accountants together!" he looks at the ghost. "Poor Dick, but of course you know that already"

"Do you recall what happened to Fezziwig and his business?"

"I think I do" Scrooge scratches his nose. "I left to set up with Jacob Marley, Dick Wilkens remained working for Fezziwig"

"And then?" the ghost pushes Scrooge for more information.

"I don't think I recall" Scrooge lies knowing that his former friend Dick Wilkens lost his position when Fezziwig was bought out by a large finance company when he could not keep up with the new competitive business environment, he also recalls that he did nothing to help his former employer or friend. He hangs his head in shame.

"Would you like to see a different past at this time, a different past for those involved?"

Scrooge thinks then replies.

"Yes, a change would be good for many hereabouts"

"Remember Ebenezer, what we are witnessing are shadows and not reality, this is the past it could have been and possibly could be"

"It can't be any worse for some" Scrooge replies.

The ghost tells Scrooge to follow Dick Wilkens, reminding him that he cannot be seen nor any interference he may wish cannot happen in this reality.

Scrooge watches as his former work colleague and friend waits outside of Fezziwig's business until he sees someone approaching.

"Tis me!" Scrooge shouts with surprise. "This is no memory I recall!"

The ghost does not answer, he points with the holly sprig at the two men, Scrooge and Wilkens who both stand outside of the building and have both removed their tall hats.

"I don't ever recall having side whiskers of such immensity!" Scrooge is excited and seems happy with what he is witnessing, he stops talking when the spirit does not engage him.

A horse drawn hearse appears at the top of the street, four black horses with high plumage on their heads slowly and with almost human solemnity move into the street gently pulling the glass sided hearse into view. The ornate coffin inside it has an off white Welsh wig atop it. Walking behind the hearse is Mrs. Fezziwig and her three daughters, Scrooge recognises one of them instantly.

"Belle" he whispers so quietly as if not wanting anyone, including himself to hear the name said out loud. "Spirit, I understand this a change to the past but who lies in the coffin?"

"You know who it is" the ghost replies without emotion.

"Fezziwig? Old Fezziwig?" Scrooge speaks with confusion in his voice. "He was so alive in the last memory you showed me, he was dancing and making merry and that joy he always had, that memory has not left me for the past decade!"

"That is your past Ebenezer, not a memory, I showed you your past and not a memory. This is a change to that past but only if you want it"

As they watch, the funeral procession passes where past Scrooge and Dick Wilkens stand with their heads bowed solemnly. Mrs. Fezziwig approaches them both and hands Scrooge several large, old fashioned keys on a thick iron ring.

"It is all yours now, yours and Dick's, he left you everything"

"Mrs. Fezziwig, Dick and I are happy for you and the young ladies to have it all, we will continue to work for you of course" Scrooge tells her and looks at his friend.

"That is true Mrs. Fezziwig, I agree wholeheartedly with Ebenezer"

Mrs. Fezziwig looks at her three bereaved daughters.

"He left us very well cared for and although we thank you from our hearts, none of us have a head for business and Nigel bequeathed it to the both of you. The business and the warehouse are now yours. May it continue to prosper under your hands"

She kisses both men on the cheek and resumes her slow walk behind the hearse, the three Fezziwig daughters follow on in silence.

"Belle..." Scrooge reaches out his hand as the oldest daughter passes, she looks up at him through tear filled eyes smiles as best she can and moves on holding the hands of her much younger siblings.

"Time passes quickly Ebenezer" the ghost speaks as the scene they are in fades and another takes its place. It is the inside of the warehouse once owned by Mr. Nigel Fezziwig but now it is the prosperous business of Scrooge and Wilkens. "Look on" the ghost instructs.

Scrooge sees himself and Dick Wilkens, older than when they were standing outside of the warehouse watching the coffin of their much loved employer passing them by, older only by a year or two, but older none the less.

"Dick is still alive! What a joy to see him older than he ever was before!" Scrooge sounds so very happy, he looks on at the scene in front of them. Younger Scrooge and the still very much alive Dick have two large ledgers open on the desk in front of them.

"Business is good Ebenezer!" Dick pats his partner on the back. "Old Fezziwig would be very proud indeed"

"The warehouse business thrives and lives on in his memory!" Ebenezer is smiling and happy, he taps the second leger. "And starting the money lending business this year has been more than a success!"

"We shall be rich Ebenezer!" Dick sounds joyous, Scrooge puts a hand on his arm.

"Money is needed Dick but it is not everything in life now is it?"

The spirit looks at old Scrooge who shrugs his shoulders.

"Your look of distain is for the old me Spirit, since your last visit I have values that agree with the much younger Ebenezer Scrooge in this memory" the ghost suddenly glows bright for a second, Scrooge chuckles. "Alright Spirit, not a memory but a past that could be!"

The spirit points to the scene unfolding in front of them.

Belle Fezziwig arrives with her mother and two sisters.

"Ebenezer! Dick! Have you not prepared for the festivities?"

Both men look at one another as a clock from outside strikes six times.

"My Lord look at the time!" Dick closes his ledger followed quickly by Ebenezer.

"We shall be ready of course ladies, we shall be on time for the annual Christmas eve party for all our staff and friends" he looks at Belle. "It will be, as always, a celebration of Mr. Fezziwig's life, he did so love a Christmas eve gathering!"

"Will you ask her tonight Ebenezer?" Dick asks his friend.

"Hush Dick!" Ebenezer scolds him. "Belle may hear you and I have not made up my mind yet"

"You are scared Ebenezer Scrooge, scared that Belle Fezziwig will turn you down!" Dick pokes fun at Scrooge who playfully punches him on the arm.

They both look up as Jacob Marley enters with a man carrying a fiddle beside him, he calls over to Scrooge.

"Ebenezer, this gentleman is here to entertain I believe"

Scrooge claps his hands together but it is Dick who approaches the musician.

"This way my friend, I do hope you know Sir Roger de Coverley, it is a tradition hereabouts on Christmas eve!"

The fiddler assures him that he is well versed in that very tune and will happily play it when instructed.

As Dick walks away to show the fiddler where to set up, Jacob approaches Scrooge.

"Ebenezer, may we speak?"

"Of course Jacob, of course!" Scrooge points to a table and hints that Jacob should take the other end for it to be moved. "What can I answer for you?"

"Will I be made a partner as the New Year arrives Ebenezer? I have worked hard and shown my dedication to you and Dick since the passing of old Fezziwig"

Scrooge puts down his end of the table whilst Jacob stands stock still with his still raised.

"Jacob, it cannot be done and for that Dick and I are sorry. We are busy and we are making money but not enough as yet for a third partner"

"You said the same last year Ebenezer" Jacob sounds angry and upset.

"I know, I know! But maybe next year Jacob, maybe next year. Come let us not talk business now, it is Christmas eve, no more work talk tonight!"

Marley drops the end of the table and it makes a loud bang.

"There will be no next year for me Ebenezer" he buttons up his jacket. "I intend to set up on my own in a different part of the city.

Dick Wilkens joins them as the noise the table made has taken his attention.

"What goes on here my merry gentlemen?" he asks trying to diffuse the tension.

Marley finishes buttoning up his jacket.

"I quit Mr. Wilkens" Marley is suddenly formal in his presentation. "I thank you and Mr. Scrooge for your generosity to me but it seems that does not extend to being a partner in this business does it?"

"Jacob. We..." Dick begins but he is cut short.

"Enjoy Christmas Eve gentlemen, I take my leave for this evening and for good!"

Marley takes his tall hat from a chair nearby, puts it on his head and walks away.

"Jacob, stay for the party please do!"

Ebenezer's words are ignored and Marley leaves with a slam of the door.

The spirit looks at Scrooge as the vision begins to fade as the fiddler begins to play.

"What is the matter?" it asks.

"Nothing in particular" said Scrooge.

"Something I think" the ghost insists.

"Not really" said Scrooge. "I should just like to have been able to say a few more words to Jacob just then. That is all"

"This is a past that has not happened as yet Ebenezer, these are visions of a past that could be"

"It is so hard Spirit, I am saddened to my very soul that Fezziwig died but I am joyous that Dick Wilkens is still alive and our business is great with customers!" his smile suddenly drops. "But to end my friendship with Jacob in this way does not sit well with me, not at all"

With a wave of the sprig of holly another room comes into vision, it is a large office with two desks on either side of it, a large bay style window gives light from outside and a view of a busy London street. Scrooge is sat at one desk and Belle is sat on his knee.

"I accept Ebenezer, I accept!" she throws her arms around his neck.

"Belle! What if someone should come in and see us?" Scrooge looks over her shoulder as she hugs him.

"I care not!" she kisses him on the cheek and stands up. "I love you Ebenezer Scrooge and accept your proposal of marriage with joy in my heart and a new fire in my belly"

Scrooge stands up and takes both her hands.

"You fulfil my life Belle, I have wanted to marry you since I first started at Fezziwig's as an apprentice. We will not be rich in money for now but know you will be rich with my love"

"Money will come my love, Scrooge and Wilkens will provide of that I am sure!" Belle moves in toward Scrooge and they maintain holding hands.

"Money is not important, my contract with you is for life, for ever, riches may come they may not, but we will always have each other"

"Your own feelings tell you that you are what you are Ebenezer, I am also and we will be one in our hearts. Through times that may be fraught and even in times of misery we will remain as one" she puts her arms around his neck once again and he puts his around her trim waist. "I will never release you Ebenezer Scrooge, never!"

"And I shall never seek release Belle, not ever"

The vision fades as suddenly as it arrived.

"Is that it?" Scrooge asks the ghost. "What happens?"

"This is a past that has not happened, so nothing happens until you will it"

Scrooge sits on the ground with his head in his hands.

"How can such happiness bring such difficulties? Belle and I are to be married and knowing I ruined it all previously it gives me great happiness to seek to amend a wrong. Business with Dick Wilkens seems to be good, again something that never happened because after I left Fezziwig's to set up with Jacob poor Dick died young" Scrooge turns to the ghost quickly as he stands up. "What happens to Jacob Marley spirit?"

"Nothing happens because this has not happened" said the ghost.

Scrooge rubs his face with both hands.

"And Fan, poor Fan, I missed my chance to see her once more" tears fall silently onto the old man's cheeks. "Dear Fan, how I wanted so much more for her"

"Always a delicate creature, whom a breath might have withered" says the Ghost. "But she had a large heart!"

"Can we go back to the school spirit, can't we just go back?"

"This is a past that has not happened Ebenezer, you cannot change what you have already asked me to take you away from"

"I know" Scrooge is sad and it shows all over his old face.

"My time with you is short Ebenezer" the ghost tells him. "I told you these were pasts of things that have not happened, but with a choice they may be"

"Remove me spirit, I cannot make a choice after such a mistake, I cannot bear it!"

With a wave of the sprig of holly the view around them changes, they are back in the countryside, it is a still, clear, cold, winter day with thick snow laying on the hardened ground.

"One more past that may be for you to see"

"Spirit? I am confused, we are back at my school again. You were insistent that my choice had been made on this matter"

"Are we at your old school Ebenezer? Look yonder, you seem to be leaving, is this perhaps a different past we are seeing?" the ghost points with the holly sprig. "Look and see"

A carriage is charging toward them, Scrooge recognises it instantly.

"This is the carriage that took me away from the school, the carriage that beautiful Fan and I took to take me back home!"

The carriage passes the spirit and Scrooge as they stand unseen on the road side, Scrooge stands on tiptoes in an attempt to see inside the carriage, for one final glimpse of his sister.

"Fan!" he calls out. "See me here Fan!" he waves his hands high above his head but the carriage charges by. "Fan" he whispers as the carriage moves out of sight.

The scene changes and Scrooge and the ghost are inside a tidy cottage kitchen, three people are sat at a scrubbed wooden table.

"Father?" Scrooge moves toward them, "Fan?"

"They cannot see you Ebenezer, you know that"

"I am with my father and sister!" Scrooge is excited, he turns to the ghost. "This is a true representation of the past, this happened, I absolutely recall it!"

"Do you?" asks the spirit.

"I do!" Scrooge replies excitedly. "This is the very Christmas I arrived home from school. My father was a much kinder man than he had been"

"He was unkind to you and to Fan" the spirit says without question in his tone.

"He was saddened by the death of my mother" Scrooge looks around the old but familiar kitchen. "She died giving birth to Fan"

"But you suffered at his hand" said the spirit, Scrooge just nods quietly. "And Fan suffered the same fate as your mother"

"As you rightly said Spirit, a delicate creature, whom a breath might have withered, she did have a large heart but not a strong one" he reaches out to touch her hair. "Dearest Fan, how I loved you so"

The vision fades and disappears, both the ghost and Scrooge have returned to the chamber of 45 Lime Street, everything is in place but it is not focused, as though it is not real.

"My time is all but over Ebenezer Scrooge and soon this journey of ours will be over, ne'er to be repeated, this room will return to reality as my light goes out" the ghost stands next to Scrooge with its light still bright but dimming by the second.

"It has to be Fan spirit, I have to choose to change Fans life if I can"

"Decisions do not have to be made as yet Ebenezer, if at all, you must remember that this is an opportunity for change but not one you have to take. You have seen how change can alter the past"

Scrooge seems in turmoil with any decision he has to make, or not as the case may be.

"If I choose Belle then Dick and darling Fan will die, that is not something I can have on my conscience"

"Fan and Dick die anyway as the past stands now Ebenezer" the ghost replies.

"I know!" Scrooge shouts, before repeating the words calmly. "I know" he shrugs his shoulders. "What do I do spirit? Whatever I do, whatever I choose, some will suffer. Can I change the past for good to the detriment of others?"

"You have that choice, none before you have had the chance to alter the past to perhaps help some"

"And to kill off others!" Scrooge shouts at the spirit who remains impassive.

"We all die, your time is soon, as is mine"

"It has to be Fan, so she can be a wife to James Holywell and a mother to Fred. It is not fair that Fred grew up without his mother" Scrooge crosses his arms over his chest.

"You did" the spirit replies.

"And look what good came of that!" Scrooge is angry and begins to cry. "Until our first meeting, until I changed toward mankind, I was a monster and ...." he does not finish his words.

"Because you blamed your mother" the spirit tells him.

Scrooge turn on the spirit quickly and with venom.

"What is that to do with you or anyone?" It is the angriest he has been for many a year and he has old risings of hatred surging through his body, he does not like these feelings and fights to rid himself of it. "It has to be Fan, I choose Fan" he says with finality.

"As you choose Ebenezer" the spirit waves his sprig of holly through the air, Scrooge is transfixed by the movement of the red berries, so much so that he does not engage when the spirit begins to fade from his view.

"I am sorry I shouted spirit, I mean nothing by it, I am thankful for both your visits" he wrings his hands together. "Although this visit has been so much more difficult than the first"

The Spirit lifts the extinguisher cone above its head and begins to lower it.

"I shall haunt you no more Ebenezer Scrooge"

"Spirit, do not leave me, I have questions that will need to be answered!" panic shows on the old man's face as the light from under the cone is very nearly gone.

"Coins Ebenezer Scrooge, do not forget the coins" these are the final words of the spirit as the light is gone and the room is plunged into darkness, the only tiny light emanates from the window in the chamber that is still not fully formed to reality.

"Is this still the past? Is this still a vision?" Scrooge cries out into the darkness. No reply is forthcoming.

Scrooge moves carefully through the pitch darkness of the room toward the window and to the light, he looks through the glass expecting to see the London Street he knows so well.

"Oh my!" he exclaims.

The silent vision below him is of three people, a man and a woman holding a tiny child, the man is knocking on his door, he hears no sound of the rapping on the knocker that once formed the face of Jacob Marley. From inside the view is one of a crisp winter day, stunning white snow, almost untouched lies on the ground, it is daylight outside but as dark as pitch in the room.

He sees himself as a younger man, still middle aged but younger than he is now, answer the door.

The silence of the world outside is matched by the words formed in his mind as the vision begins to fade"

"Thank you my love" Scrooges own voice passes through his head without him moving his lips.

"What for Brother?" he hears Fan speak to him for the first time in many a year.

"For all of this" he sees himself wave at the winter scene then he puts a hand on her shoulder and gently lifts the blankets of the bundle she is carrying, he knows it is Fred as a baby. "For all of this"

He can hear the joy and happiness in his voice as the vision fades and the world outside of the window returns to the darkness of night.

A candle ignites on the mantle above the fire and the fire itself glows red again bringing warmth and welcome low light to the chamber. He is back and the visions and the ghost are all in the past of the night.

"Was it real? Will she be back to see me again Spirit, tell me that and nothing more?"

The many small spits and crackles from the fire are the only sounds that answer him, he bends down and adds a shovel of coal to the glowing red embers and blows gently upon them to encourage flame and much needed heat, after the brightness of the spirit the room begins to feels dull and cold.

Scrooge remembers the words of the spirit, 'Coins Ebenezer Scrooge, do not forget the coins'. He leaves the warm chamber with the candle burning in the holder now in his hands and steps into the hallway, slowly he walks down the stairs until he reaches the stand where his jacket hangs. He takes the coins from the pocket, the coins he removed from the dead eyes of Jacob Marley so many years before, they sit coldly in the palm of his hand.

"I so fear what these pennies may mean for me" he speaks to the darkness that surrounds him.

Stave III

Ghost of Christmas Presents

Scrooge reaches the top of the stairs and he can see light forcing its way out from under his chamber door, momentary panic seizes him as he fears that the fire has spat out a burning coal and the room is alight.

"Humbug Scrooge! Coal cannot have gotten that hot in the few minutes since I left" he says to himself.

He rubs the coins in his left hand and puts them into his dressing gown pocket, raising the candle he opens the door to his chamber.

He opens his mouth to scream as the door opens but no sound comes out.

"Come in an know me better man!" a booming voice passes across the chamber.

Scrooge steps inside and closes the door, the room is not afire from a stray coal or ember but it is changed, the sight is a familiar one to him, from a memory from another time past.

"Spirit?" he says quietly.

"Come in and know me better man!" the giant ghost calls out in a very jolly voice. "I am the ghost of Christmas Presents, look upon me!"

Scrooge blows out the candle as it is no longer needed as a mighty blaze is now alight in the fireplace, many candles are lit around the room and the spirit carries the same glowing torch resembling Plenty's horn as his predecessor had. It is his own room, of that there is now doubt, but just as before it its transformed, the walls and ceiling are alive with green vines and holly with vivid gleaming red berries a plenty, mistletoe is hung in amounts such as Scrooge as never seen and the pure whiteness of their fruit reflect the light from the fire and the Spirits torch as if hundreds of tiny mirrors have been placed upon every surface. The giant ghost is sat upon a throne made of turkey, geese and all other poultry, brawn alongside huge joints of meat with sucking pigs and links of sausage forming the arms. About the feet of the ghost sits mince pies, plum puddings, steaming paper bags of chestnuts and bowls of the reddest apples alongside juicy oranges and luscious pears. Several huge twelfth night cakes are scattered amongst the fruits and nuts, Scrooge closes his eyes and sniffs deeply though his nose believing he can smell the deep aroma of the leavened bread cake filled with ale soaked fruit.

The giant ghost sits comfortably on the throne amongst the masses of food, he looks similar if not exactly the same as the 1843 ghost of Christmas Present, he is dressed simply in a green robe bordered with white fur, it hangs loosely on the immense figure of the ghost so that the abundant breast of him is open for all to see. A belt is girded around the ample middle of the giant and attached to it is a swordless antique and rusted scabbard, exactly the same as the previous ghost of this incarnation, he is shoeless and upon his head, atop his bright red hair is a crown of ivy, his beard is wild and as red as his hair.

"I know who you are spirit, we have met before" Scrooge speaks without moving from where he stands.

"Not me! We have never met of that I am certain!" the ghost laughs so loud that the very foundations of the house seem to shake. "You have never seen the like of me before!"

"I think I have Spirit, we are reacquainted, you visited me in this very room on the eve before Christmas day in the year of our Lord 1843"

The spirit tilts his head toward Scrooge, small leaves of ivy fall to the ground from the crown he wears.

"I do not think so, maybe you walked forth with younger members of my family whom I have never walked with but they are now my older brothers born from earlier years!"

"More than eighteen hundred if I recall" Scrooge says with a smile on his face. "Eighteen hundred and fifty two before you"

Raucous laughter emanates through the room as the ghost throws back his head with gusto.

"That is so! You have met my brothers!"

"Brother" replies Scrooge. "Just the one brother and he had brown hair and a crown of holly as I recall spirit" Scrooge says and is happy with his observation.

The spirit lifts the glowing torch as had his brother before him, he points around the room with it.

"I have spruced up the drabness of your home. Why not a single festive decoration about the place?"

"Spirit, do not think of me as mean or parsimonious, it is just that this year I am spending the season firstly with my senior clerk and his family and then to my nephew for the Feast of Stephen celebrations, this is not a miserly decision but more one of practicality as I will not be here"

"Then I am glad I am able to add light and joy to your life!"

"Oh I can assure you Spirit, your brother before you and the other spirits certainly did that for me and I have carried both in my heart ever since"

"I have two present times for us to visit this night" the ghost is suddenly serious and quite stern.

"Two?" asks Scrooge. "The same as before with your brother?"

The ghost shakes his enormous head and laughs so very loud that the floor seems to shake.

"Two presents for two visits, one as it is now as things are and the other with changes" he points the flaming torch at Scrooge. "Changes you made, your decisions and your choices made in good faith and with humanity in mind"

"Have the changes been made Spirit?" Scrooge asks.

"Change is exactly that is it not? Decisions made, changes made, is that not what you asked for?"

"I did" Scrooge is firm in his answer. "Shall I take your robe Spirit as we did before?"

The ghost throws his head back and its long curly red hair moves freely as he laughs and laughs.

"I believe you have a small task with coins to complete first do you not?" he stands and points at the bedside stand. Scrooge bows his head.

"I do, but I fear it Spirit"

"Do not fear what cannot be changed man, only fear what you can change for it can alter the lives of many or none at all" the ghost replies as he sits down. "We shall not move on until the set task is complete"

Scrooge takes the two pennies from his dressing gown pocket and places them on the small table beside his bed, the face of King William IV looks up at him in the gloom. The giant ghost stands up and steps down beside Scrooge.

"Now you may touch my robe, we have much to see, much to learn and very little time for it all"

Scrooge reaches forward and grabs a handful of the green robes as the Spirit waves the lighted torch around his head making sparks and stars fly around the room, Scrooge is feared that not for the first time that evening, that his chamber may catch fire.

Almost immediately they are both inside the home of the Cratchit family, number two Lime Street, Scrooge claps his hands.

"The home of Bob Cratchit! I have been here many a time" he looks up at the ghost. "This is a very different vision from when I visited the old Cratchit house with your brother" Scrooge scratches his chin. "We visited the chimneys and the poor houses in the city, we visited the grocers, then the richest in town and those flocking to prayer!"

"Different times, I am not my brother, although I will bless the poor as he surely did" the torch is waved again around his head.

"Because the poor need it most" Scrooge whispers so as not to be heard.

"And because there are still those on this earth of yours who lay claim to know me and my kind, many are filled with ill-will, hatred and bigotry, they are as they always have been, as strange to us and all our kin as if they had never lived."

Scrooge nods as if in agreement, the speech from the giant ghost is similar to that of this brother, Scrooge had to confess quietly to himself that he had little understanding of it then and nothing much has changed over the years that have prevailed.

"Does that mean that those of religion might have un Christian attitudes toward others, those that mean well?"

"Not all but some. These ideals have not changed for hundreds of years in the past, their immorality is not my business, but those who claim justification for their actions will continue to live their own lives as strangers to the true meaning of this time of year and I doubt they will change in the future" he looks at Scrooge. "The future is not my business"

A shiver forms and moves down the spine of the old man as he recalls the third ghost he met previously.

"I think I understand Spirit and I am glad to my soul that we are in the home of Bob Cratchit"

"Look on, this is the present, this is right now"

"We cannot be seen or heard?" Scrooge asks.

"No, not now nor at any time" the spirit waves his torch and more sparks and stars fly about the house. "I bless the home of Bob Cratchit and his family"

Both men look on, unseen by Emily and Tim who are in the kitchen.

"Where is your Father Tim? He always disappears on Christmas eve when there are chores to be done"

"Decorating the tree in the dining room Mother, you know how he gets!"

"He better not forget to stoke the coals in the oven tonight, I need it hot for first thing to get the dinner cooked. The goose has to go to the bakers very soon, my it is a monster!"

Tim laughs and pushes himself up using his stick.

"I should go and help Father put up the decorations for the celebration tomorrow"

Both look up as the kitchen door is knocked and then opened before either of them can shout 'Come in!'

Martha steps in covered in snow.

"God love us the weather is worsening!"

"Martha!" Tim is so happy to see his sister.

Martha's husband, Joe, walks in behind her with two children in his arms, Scrooge nudges the spirit.

"That is young David, or Davey as I call him, he is four years old and his younger sister is just two years old and she is known to us all as Little Jane"

Scrooge has his chest puffed out with pride, the ghost has a smile on his face as they both look on at the scene in front of them.

"Joseph Blake put those children down and show me your hands!" Emily demands of her son in law.

"Mother!" Martha protests. "My Joe is clean as a whistle"

"All is well Martha my love" Joe giggles as he shows Emily his clean scrubbed hands, she checks both sides.

"You need gloves Joseph, your hands are cold but for a grimy coal merchant you are clean enough!"

He leans forward and kisses Emily on the cheek.

"Thank you mother in law" he puts his arm around her waist.

"Enough of that! I have work to do and lots to prepare for tomorrow" she turns to her grandchildren. "Go to the dining room, I am certain Grandpa will let you help him dress the tree!"

"I will take them, come on both of you"

Tim puts his stick under his arm and holds out both his hands and David and Little Jane take hold.

"Will we have gifts Uncle Tim?" Little Jane asks.

"Only if you have been good!" Tim declares.

"Oh" Little Jane replies sounding downhearted.

"All will be well Little Jane I am certain of it. Come along"

Tim leads both the children from the kitchen they can be heard cheering and laughing all the way until both children can be heard to shout, in the loudest of voices. 'Surprise Grandpa!'

"Will Uncle Ebenezer be attending for lunch tomorrow Mother?" Martha asks.

"The old miser will be here of that you can be sure Martha!"

"Emily, you are such a horror to dear Mr. Scrooge" Joe laughs as he takes off his hat, coat and scarf.

"Hang them neatly if you please Joseph!" Emily tells him. "And you did not know the old Scrooge as I did!"

Martha hugs her mother tightly.

"We all remember him as he was Mother, but what a fine man he has become, what a great friend and a second father not only to Tim but to David and Little Jane. They all love him so!"

"As do I" Emily is trying to be stern but a smile is creeping onto her lips. "But it doesn't hurt for him to be reminded"

Scrooge looks up at the ghost with a huge grin on his face, the ghost waves his hand instructing the old man to continue to watch.

The three of them are disturbed by a raucous rendition of 'Hark the Herald Angels Sing' that is coming from the dining room and is getting nearer and nearer to the kitchen until Bob, Tim, David and Little Jane burst in all singing their hearts out!

When they have finished, mainly because David and Little Jane have forgotten the words, a round of applause breaks out and the children cheer loudly. Bob puts his arms around Martha.

"Merry Christmas my Martha, it is so lovely to see you all here in this house, it makes it full and alive as it always should be!"

"Are you sure we can stay the night Sir?" Joe steps forward and shakes hands with Bob.

"Of course it is! We have plenty of room" he looks at Emily. "Not like the old place"

Emily sighs.

"Agreed Robert, but I did so love that old house of ours, it was a bit tatty and oh so small for all of us but we had happy times there did we not"

"We did my love, but living here rent free as part of my position at Scrooge and Marley is a marked step up for us all" he seems momentarily melancholic. "Although we won't all be here again this Christmas"

Emily dusts flour from her hands and takes Bobs in hers.

"Now you listen here Robert Cratchit, our son and your heir is serving Queen and country, he will be home soon and then we can have a Christmas together again"

"I know that my love, it is just I want us all to be here, our family, the grandchildren and Mr. Scrooge, all here to celebrate another year of happiness"

"Peter will be home soon" Martha tells them all. "His last letter told that his ship, HMS Hermes is preparing to steam back to England early next year"

"Will we ever meet Uncle Peter Mummy?" Little Jane asks. Bob picks her up and squeezes her until she giggles.

"Of course you will, before you know it!"

"Is Uncle Peter as old as Uncle Ebenezer?" David asks.

Everyone laughs long and loud until Belinda comes in through the kitchen door.

"Have I missed a joke?" she asks them all.

Emily rushes over and kisses her daughter and helps her off with her coat.

"Not at all, young David was comparing your brother to Ebenezer!"

"Oh dear!" Belinda gasps. "Albie will hope to be here the day after tomorrow Mother, he is on duty at the palace all day today and tomorrow"

"Your Uncle Albert is a footman to the Queen!" Bob tells both his grandchildren as the others groan.

"Father, you always tell the children every time my husband is mentioned!" Belinda greets her father with a hug. "Her Majesty is staying at Osbourne House for Christmas, Albie did not travel and is at the palace for the duration"

"You are cold Belinda, here step in by the fireplace" he ushers her nearer to the warmth. "Your Albert drawn the short straw for Christmas duty?"

She nods.

"Again!" she moans then smiles. "I do have some news for you all" she rubs her tummy gently. Emily screams with happiness and Bob claps his hands.

"Belinda! A baby! How marvellous, the best present at Christmas!"

The rest of the family fuss over her and make her sit down until she begs them all for silence.

"I must ask one thing from you all, please let me tell Uncle Scrooge when he arrives tomorrow, you know how he dotes on all of us so, especially the children"

They all agree to keep the secret from him until Belinda can tell him personally. Bob bangs on the table with his fist.

"Joe, if you please could you hand out a glass of punch to each and every one of us" he looks at David and Little Jane. "Well, nearly everyone!"

Joe plunges the ladle into the bowl of punch on the wood burning range stove and hands out a mug to all present, Bob stands on a chair.

"Raise your glasses one and all to the founder of our Christmas feast, our good friend Mr. Ebenezer Scrooge"

"Mr. Scrooge!" they all say in unison.

They all stand for a few moments in reflective silence. Bob breaks it.

"Mrs. Cratchit, I do hope the Christmas pudding is as good if not better than last year's triumph!"

They all cheer and raise their glasses once more.

"Time for us to leave" the ghost tells Scrooge.

"Can we not stay just for one more moment?"

"Time to move on, we have much to see" the ghost insists.

"I will be back tomorrow, I will not breath a word of what I have seen here, especially the news of Belinda being with child. How exciting!"

The ghost does not answer Scrooge, they leave as the happy household are drinking punch and singing more carols. Scrooge feels happy and is looking forward to the day tomorrow, despite his earlier news from the ghost of Jacob Marley, he feels satisfied and calm.

"Where do you take me spirit?" Scrooge asks as they walk through familiar London Streets, he notes a hint of greyness in the beard of the ghost, he does not mention it. "Are we headed back to my chambers?"

The giant ghost chuckles gleefully.

"Did you ask as many questions of my brother so many years ago?"

"I believe I may have" Scrooge stops and clicks his fingers. "I have it! Your brother took me to a bleak and desolate moor, to visit miners and a family living in a house made of mud and stone, then onto those that are keepers of the lighthouse and finally onto a sailing ship on high seas!"

"You already know how those souls keep Christmas, those are images from your past and that past is as it is. Your present is now and if it changes it is because you have willed it. Those images are as they are and always have been"

"I am confused Spirit, last time I was to be shown the suffering of others, the poverty of others against the vast wealth of some. I have shown compassion and happiness, I have shown charity. Any change I wish for are for Fan and for her life"

"Happiness costs nothing, charity costs little but doing nothing can cost dearly" the ghost tells him.

"Are you telling me that change is good or bad? I don't understand why I am being shown this present when there is nothing that needs to be changed?"

It is getting very dark as they walk, it is snowing heavily and as they pass the brightness of roaring fires in kitchens and parlours, Scrooge feels a warmth and happiness that goes against the wintery scene they are in. He sees families from all parts of London society preparing dinner for a cosy and warm Christmas eve, children are running in the streets and sliding on the snow ignoring how wet and cold their boots and clothes have become, Scrooge waves but not one of them see him. They pass through an alleyway and the world around them suddenly changes, the houses are smaller, closer together and black with grime, the smell coming from the gutter is enough to turn any mans stomach. None of the houses have the flicker of warm flame from a fire or an oven in a kitchen, all are dark and subdued, children are also outside just as they had been a street or two away but there is no fun sliding and playing in the snow. These children are ragged and each one looks hungry and cold, Scrooge reaches into his dressing gown pocket hoping to find a coin or two for them to share.

"Your money is no good here" the ghost tells him, his beard and hair now having as much grey and white as red within it. "These children are mankind's secret, kept away from decent society, they are want and ignorance, angels have forsaken them and devils lurk in wait"

"I was told to beware ten years ago Spirit, to beware them and all their degree. I have slandered all who told it, I have admitted mistakes and I have championed the poor and the needy!"

"But still they have no refuge or resource" the ghost cries out as though in pain.

"Only the prisons and workhouses Spirit and they are factious places and make any bad situation worse" Scrooge looks up at the ghost in an attempt to assist in reducing the pain on his face.

"I am pleased you are appalled and I am satisfied that you have made some amends to changing lives"

"This is bigger than me Spirit" it is Scrooges turn to feel internal dismay and pain.

"You know this place?" the giant asks him, his face slightly sagged and wrinkled as he points a house that is well lit in the winter darkness.

"Know it! I spent last Christmas here and many Sundays for dinner over the years with Fred and Lily!" Scrooge puffs out his chest for the second time that evening. "I have the real pleasure to say that Fred purchased this house himself, despite my offer of financial assistance, he refused. He has never wanted a penny from me"

With a wave of the torch Scrooge and the ghost are transported inside, Fred is kneeling by the fireplace and Lily has three stockings on her lap.

"I bless this house and all who live in it" the ghost speaks but only Scrooge can hear him, the stars and sprinkles emit from the torch as he moves it around.

"We have spoilt the children this year Fred, I am certain that these old stockings will be fit to bursting or not substantial enough for everything!"

Fred sits upright on his knees.

"My love, I have worked hard keeping books for many small businesses in and around the city, income is steady and I am glad to say that it has increased over the past few years"

"Since Uncle Ebenezer took you on!"

Fred feigns shock and puts his hand on his heart.

"Say no more dear wife, you hurt me so!"

She puts her hand to her mouth to stifle a laugh.

"Oh Fred, you are as funny and charming as the day we met"

"Put the gifts in the stockings Emily so I can hang them on the mantle"

Emily puts an orange, small packets of bon bons and humbugs and a packet of nuts into each stocking before handing them to Fred.

"We also have a book for each of the children, although I know Frances is very young I want our children to own literature for their future"

"I have a confession to make" Fred reaches behind a straight backed chair and brings out a paper sack.

"Frederick Holywell what do you have there?" she puts the stockings down on the cushion next to her.

"Surprises!" Fred cheers, he reaches into the sack and brings out already wrapped gifts. "Toy soldiers for Samuel, included are tiny pots of paint for him to decorate them" Emily raises her eyebrows. "For Noah I have a super spinning top and for Frances I have a small dolly with a rather fetching change of clothes!"

"She is just three Fred!"

He laughs a long and happy laugh.

"It's Christmas Mrs. Holywell" he takes out one more small parcel, wrapped in expensive, thick paper, he hangs it gently on a branch of the small but fabulously decorated Christmas tree. "And this if for you"

She stands up knocking one of the stockings to the floor.

"For me! What is it?" she demands happily.

"That is to be seen tomorrow my love, you will have to be patient"

Emily picks up the fallen stocking and hands it to her husband who hangs it on the small nail he has already fixed into the wooden mantle above the fire, this is repeated twice more in silence. They both stand back and admire their work.

"I have a small gift for Uncle Ebenezer" Fred tells Emily who puts her hand to her mouth.

"So have I Fred!" she giggles through her hands.

"We will have such a fabulous feast day with him, he will so love his gifts. What have you got him?" Fred asks her.

"Not telling!" she pushes him playfully.

"He has been so very kind to us and generous to the children, he loves them as if they were his very own"

"I agree Fred, since his change all those years ago, and what a change it was and what a surprise when he arrived for Christmas dinner that day!"

"1843" Fred says quietly. "The very next year, on the first month of 1844 he purchased almost every house at Baynham Street and I have managed them for him ever since. He never interferes and he never questions my figures"

"I am certain you are a fair and honest man Fred Holywell!"

"I am and proud to be so but Uncle Ebenezer is very good to his tenants, the houses are as good as they can be and the rent is as low as it can be, certainly lower than many others in Camden Town"

Fred stands and pours two large sherries into crystal glasses, he hands one to Emily.

"To Uncle Ebenezer, the founder of our fortune..."

"Not quite a fortune Fred!" Emily barges into his words but stops when he scowls at her playfully.

"To Uncle Ebenezer, the founder of our comfort" he pokes his tongue out at Emily who gasps with a sharp intake of breath. "May he know he is always welcome in our house and we will always let him in. As good a man as this city has ever seen and ever will I think"

"Bravo! We shall all miss him tomorrow, we shall miss him greatly" Emily sips at her sherry and looks at Fred over the top of the small glass. "I shall ask Topper and my sister tomorrow what gift you have for me"

"They are sworn to secrecy and you shall have to wait until after dinner to see what it is" Fred taps the side of his head suddenly. "I have a brilliant idea my dear!"

"Do you mean me asking Topper or Victoria what gift you have purchased for me?"

"I shall take it back if you even think about cheating and trying to steal a view by tearing a small fragment of paper from it!' he sips his sherry and sits down next to his wife. "Shall we walk the children to the Cratchits house after dinner tomorrow? I know Topper, Victoria and baby Thomas would love to see them all, especially Uncle Ebenezer"

"I feel Mr. and Mrs. Cratchit will not be ready to receive guests and we may appear rude"

"Bob and Emily will not mind one little bit I am certain of it!" Fred claps his hands with joy. "We can take some festive cheer, wine and fruit jellies, unless Topper eats all of them before dinner!"

Emily sips at her Sherry again, she puts the glass down on the small table next to where she is seated.

"A splendid idea husband! I am so looking forward to seeing the look on Uncle Ebenezer's face when we all arrive!"

Fred leans in and kisses his wife on the lips.

"Merry Christmas Emily my love"

"Fred!" she sounds surprised but quickly returns the kiss. "Merry Christmas Husband"

The scene fades and Scrooge and the ghost are back in his chamber, it is warm as it was when they left.

"You grow old Spirit as your brother did before you"

"Time waits for no man or ghost so we must move on"

"Move on? To where? I have seen this Christmas present and I am very satisfied with the lives of my friends and family. Tomorrow will be a splendid day especially now I know that Fred, Emily and the children will be surprising the Cratchits! It will be so joyous with much singing, dancing and eating!" he puts his finger to his lips. "Our secret spirit, I will take it to the grave"

"And you will I am sure" the giant speaks quietly to Scrooge who understands fully the meaning of the ghosts words.

"But Fan is still dead" Scrooge cries suddenly. "In this very moment, in this very reality, she is not alive!" he wipes tears from his face. "The ghost of Christmas past informed me that the past is the past and I and I alone have the opportunity to change it, the only man ever to have this offer. I opted for Fan to live, to survive again, but it seems that these are shadows that the past may keep forever"

The ghost waves his torch, still burning but not as fiercely as when he arrived, sparks and stars flicker from its flames.

"She lives" the ghost says with his hand on his heart.

"Take my robe, we have more to see"

Although confusion has taken over his every being, he does as instructed by the ever ageing ghost.

The chamber slowly disappears again and the vision becomes one that is as familiar to Scrooge as any he can recall.

"Spirit? This is number sixteen Bayham Street, the former home of my senior clerk, Bob Cratchit"

"This is the present as you requested, the present with Fan not dying whilst giving life to your nephew. This is your choice and this is the present you have brought to life"

The ghost moves to the door of the house, Scrooge seems frozen to where he stands.

"I cannot" Scrooge whispers.

"You shall, this is your choice, you shall see what it has done for better or worse!"

Scrooge reluctantly follows the ghost through the shabby front door and into one of the two rooms downstairs, it is empty bar a few pieces of shabby furniture, the fire lies dull and silent despite the coldness of the day outside. The ghost points toward the other room, a room that Scrooge knows is the kitchen, he walks as though in pain, not wanting to see what awaits him.

The fire is lit in the small room although only just, the warmth is minimal, Emily Cratchit sits at the table with Martha, Peter and Belinda on harsh wooden chairs, two seats remain untaken.

"Peter is serving in the Queens navy spirit, Martha is married to Joe Blake a coal merchant, I went to their wedding, they have children, Davey and Little Jane. Belinda is with child and everyone is so excited for her and Albert. I know them all so well"

They are all as old as they should be but quite different to those he witnessed just a short time ago. Emily is dressed in a well-worn gown that is held together in places by patches of different colours and materials, she is clean and tidy with frayed ribbons in her hair and holes in her shoes.

"I have not made a pudding for this year, I just cannot face it" she cries into her hands.

"Fear not Mother" Martha puts her hand on Emily's arm to comfort her. "All will be well this Christmas eve, Peter and Belinda will leave soonest for the market, we have a few copper coins if we need them but we hope for luck and the generosity of the stall holders who will only throw away the produce if we don't take it from them"

"We have been greatly lucky before Mother and we can do it again" Peter tells them all.

Belinda is silent and begins to sob after looking at the corner of the room next to the fire.

There standing on its own is a small crutch, the type of crutch a child would use if for example, they had crippled legs.

Scrooge is wide eyed and points at the corner.

"Spirit, tell me not bad news, tell me the child I think that belongs to is alive to this very day"

"I see empty chairs at this table, if these shadows remain as they are then the crutch that has remained unused for some time will remain where it is for time immemorial"

"I have seen the future Spirit, I have lived it to this very day. Tim does have a future as does the whole of the Cratchit family. Everything I have will be theirs!" he pleads to the ghost. "How can things in this present be so bad with such positive changes to the past?"

The ghost remains silent and waves his torch, his arms are thin and his face craggy, he seems tired as he lifts the torch, the vision of the Cratchits kitchen thankfully fades from Scrooges view.

"I love you but perhaps we should never have married Ebenezer" Belle speaks with sternness in her voice, any memory of her soft loving tones are gone from this vision.

Scrooge looks at his own self seated at the desk at Fezziwig's warehouse, he looks very much as he does now.

"Spirit, what does she mean? I have confusion in my mind, fog in my soul. The past I visited earlier gave me the option to marry and I chose Fan over Belle"

The spirit looks at Ebenezer and sighs.

"Because you did not choose to marry Belle, it does not mean that you didn't"

Scrooge puts his fists into his eyes.

"No! I am not understanding this at all. What is happening?"

"Look on and listen, out time together moves on with haste"

Scrooge stands back with the ghost and observes as this new present unfolds in front of them.

Belle takes off her wedding ring and puts it on the desk.

"My heart is broken Ebenezer, we married for love when we had nothing and we were happy"

"I am still happy!"

"Happy at work, you are obsessed with it all! This is a thriving business, Scrooge and Wilkens has become a success but to what cost?"

"Comfort and happiness take time and dedication Belle, come now, calm down and return to our home, I will be along shortly"

"When? I sit at home night after night, week after week and month and year after month after another year and I am alone!" she pounds the desk angrily. "I married you for love Ebenezer Scrooge not for money, not for business but for you, I wanted to be with you"

"And I you my love" he insists. "But since Dick left the business..."

"Left?" she laughs in between her tears. "Left? You bought him out did you not? He could no longer keep up with your obsession and demands about money, he wanted to help people, to help those in need"

"So did I!" Scrooge shouts at his wife. "I always lend money to those who need it"

"At what cost Ebenezer? You took their houses, their property, their lives and their very souls when they could not repay you. Dick wanted to be charitable, to be generous but you wanted money, more and more money!"

"It makes for good business Belle, for a good family life"

Belle wipes her tears away and becomes momentarily calm, a calmness that both the Scrooges present felt uncomfortable being around.

"We have no family Ebenezer, this is your family" she waves at the warehouse. "You promise me children, you promise trips to nice restaurants, to the seaside but never have you delivered!"

"If you leave you will have nothing, not a penny" he says to her angrily.

"I need not your money Ebenezer, I need my life and I need my sanity, neither of which you can buy for me!"

'Belle" Scrooge stands up and tries to be calm with his wife. "I do love you so"

"Goodbye Ebenezer, we shall see each other no more"

Belle turns on her heels and leaves the room slamming the door behind her.

Ebenezer Scrooge makes no attempt to follow her.

The spirit looks at the scene without catching Scrooges eye.

"Get after her you fool!" Scrooge shouts at his present self. "Get up and chase what you really want and not what you need, we have messed this up before and it does not make for a happy life!"

"He cannot hear you" the ghost says without any happiness in his voice.

The torch is waved again but without being raised above the old spirits head, the scene changes and they move on.

"This is Fred's old house, where he lived with Lily before he moved to Leadenhall Street" Scrooge speaks to the spirit who seems to be ignoring him, he has his hand to his large chest. "Are you quite well spirit?" Scrooge asks.

"I grow old, my time on this earth is short, some spirits live for a long time, even forever but my life is short" he looks at Scrooge. "My life ends at midnight and I may not be alone"

Scrooge refuses to be drawn into a conversation about death.

"Why are we visiting Fred's former residence?" he asks after changing the subject.

"Former residence? This is the home of Mr and Mrs Fred Holywell and their three children"

"Samuel, Noah and darling Fan" Scrooge speaks almost in a whisper, he clears his throat before continuing. "They live at number one Leadenhall Street, I know this because I offered Fred assistance to buy it and he as usual refused and purchased it through hard work and savings. He is a fine man whom I am proud to know"

"He is a fine man indeed, but in this changed present he has not moved and still lives in this very house" with difficulty he waves the barely lit torch. "Let us look inside"

The view changes slowly and the spirit and Scrooge are transported into a small but warm and comfortable living room, Fred and Lily are not alone, also present are Lilys sister Victoria and her husband John 'Topper' Haines, a long-time friend of Fred's who is singing in a loud bass voice as Lily plays the piano.

"Shy, shy, shy, shy, Oh! I'm shy—dreadfully shy. Shy, shy, shy, shy, When I put on the ring, I was awfully shy!" he finishes the tune with a flourish of his hand and an over dramatic bow.

"Bravo Topper, bravo!" Fred is on his feet and clapping loudly.

"Hush Fred!" scolds Lily. "You will awaken the children"

"It will take more than singing and clapping to wake Thomas, he is such a good sleeper" Victoria speaks from her seat next to the roaring fire.

"Not so our three, they all stated earlier that they were not going to sleep at all this Christmas eve!"

"I do believe I sang that very song to you before we were wed my love" Topper speaks to his wife.

"I do believe you and Fred also nicknamed me 'the plump one' did you not?"

Fred and Topper laugh and look at Lily knowingly.

"It was not me!" Lily looks at her sister. "I did not give you any such name, Victoria do not believe these buffoons!"

"We played blind man's bluff and Topper cheated so that he could catch Victoria!" Fred laughs as he talks.

"And your Uncle Scrooge failed to appear as he always has!" Topper screams with delight.

"I bet Fred asked him again this year didn't you Fred?" Victoria asks.

As Fred ponders an answer, Scrooge turns to the spirit who appears to be half asleep, his hair now almost completely grey and white, a few rebellious red strands stand out in his beard.

"I did turn up! It was my first Christmas with my Nephew and Lily! I recall it well"

"Not in this present, you did not appear" he points back at the living room scene.

"I wish he would you know, I am sure it would do him so good in his heart to see the children so excited, to see Topper and Victoria, to meet Thomas our newest member of this family!"

"He won't Fred, he never has and he never will" Lily touches he husbands arm gently.

Scrooge is feeling angry and more than a little frightened with the unfolding scene in front of him.

"I was here, with your brother some ten years ago" he screws his eyes up and thinks hard. "They played the yes and no game, Fred was playing and the others had to guess what he was thinking of. It was an animal!" Scrooge is suddenly smiling and seemingly happy. "It was live and disagreeable, a savage beast that growled and grunted and lived here in London where it walked the streets! It was never led by others and did not live in a menagerie and was never killed at market" Scrooge continues with his eyes still screwed tightly shut. "Not a horse or a cow, nor a bull or tiger, dog, pig, cat or bear! Victoria guessed it, she guessed correctly!"

"What was the animal in question?" the ghost ask weakly.

"It was I" Scrooges happiness leaves him instantly. "It was I, Uncle Scrooge, the butt of the joke" he hangs his head onto his chest.

"Look on, there is more to see"

"I wish to see no more spirit, take me from here"

The ghost points at the scene and for the first time he has anger in his tone.

"Look on!"

Scrooge turns back to the scene without further question, Topper is holding his heart with both hands and looking at his wife.

"How is he so perfect? Thomas is so perfect, born from a beauty and he is a beauty!"

Victoria blushes.

"Topper Haines, you always know how to make me feel nice and embarrassed at the same time" Topper raises his eyebrows at her. "Topper! Don't be so!"

Lily speaks to Fred gently.

"Your mother would have so loved to have met even one of her grandchildren and to see her brother as a fine and successful man"

"She is so always here in my heart. She was always a delicate creature, whom a breath might have withered, but she had a large heart"

He takes Lily's hand and kisses it gently.

"She missed your Father so much I believe?" she talks gently to him.

"He died when I was young so my memory of him has faded to all but nothing" he kisses his wife's hand again. "Enough melancholy! Music Lily if you please. Topper, a festive carol if you please"

Topper Haines looks at Lily and winks.

"Well as it happens, Lily and I have been secretly practicing a new carol for Christmas, we hoped you would want us to sing!"

Victoria and Fred both clap their hands and encourage the carol to begin, Lily takes a sheet of music from a book on top of the piano, it is crisp and new.

"I do hope I can play it well"

"Come along, we can do it! The name of the carol is 'Good King Wenceslas" Topper stands behind her as she takes her seat at the piano. She begins to play and the vision begins to mist over and blur in front of Scrooges eyes.

"Must we go Spirit, I have not heard this new carol and would like to stay"

"Did you hear the conversation?" the ghost asks as he coughs and splutters and struggles for breath.

"I did but I want to ignore it, I want to pretend I did not hear it as I thought I had"

"You heard right and we both know it" more coughing from the giant spirit who is now diminutive in his posture and size.

Scrooge looks up and wails at the ghost.

"Fan is dead! After all this she is dead anyway!"

"Some are just not for saving Ebenezer" the ghost speaks rapidly and breathlessly, he uses Scrooges name for the first time the old man can recall.

"How long did she live for in this present Spirit?" he begs to know. "Did she have a lovely life? I saved her did I not?"

"For as long as your God would let her" the ghost says as he sits on the ground obviously exhausted.

"I saved her from an early grave! I saved her, it was my choice, I told the ghost of Christmas past! It was my choice and the correct choice" he clenches his fists. "The other choices came to some form of the truth anyway!" Scrooge is angry and shouting at the ghost who shakes his head weakly.

"Sacrifice and decisions are always difficult" the quickly ageing spirit tells Scrooge.

"Did I make the right one? Would my Fan have lived any longer if my decision was different? I never married and eventually became happy with my life and friends" he stands over the ghost who is lying on the ground. "I recall Belle did marry without me and lived a full and happy life, the first ghost all those years ago told me so. What decision should I have made Spirit? What should I have done for all to be right at this the time of goodwill to all?"

The ghost does not answer, he has spent his last seconds on earth and dies to dust as a faraway church clock chimes, the

Ghost of Christmas Presents blows away on the night breeze in front of Scrooges eyes as darkness falls around the world they are in at that very moment, he closes his eyes tightly and silently sobs in the pitch black that surrounds him.

Stave IV

Ghost of Christmas Yet To Come.

The chamber is dark when Scrooge opens his eyes but not so dark as to be blind and to be fumbling around, the fire is still aglow and the candle, although nearly spent, burns its final breath on the mantle.

The shadows in one corner of the room begin to grow and to take the form of a ghost that makes Scrooge take a deep intake of breath as the phantom approaches in silence.

"We meet again Spirit" he says with a calmness to his voice that surprises him. "What do you show me? The time yet to come as I previously knew it?"

The ghost moves its hooded face from side to side, Scrooge moves to be as far away from the ghost as he can be in the room.

"You are here to show me the future as I have changed it? With Fan's life not being snuffed out as she breathed life into Fred?" The hood moves up and down in a positive gesture. "I was afraid of that" Scrooge says quietly, almost whispering as though a scared child.

The black shroud around the unseen body of this ghost drapes heavily over a secretive frame, the hood conceals completely the head and face and as hard as Scrooge stares all he can see is an endless darkness that gives him a feeling of solemn dread that surrounds the mystery of the foreboding ghost.

"You are the spirit of Christmas Yet To Come."

No answer is made by the ghost but a ghastly hand appears from the shroud and points at Scrooge.

"You are here to show me the shadows of things that have not happened but of those that will happen in time before us. Time it seems I have influenced?"

Scrooge looks for a nodding movement from the hood of the ghost but receives nothing to indicate any answer to his question.

"Ghost of the future!" Scrooge speaks with bravery in his tone. "I feared you more than all the other spectres previously, but I do not fear you as I did. I hope to live, to continue my life as it is, to see good in others and to help who I can. I do fear that this may not be the truth I will receive from you"

As in its previous incarnation the silent ghost points an almost skeletal hand straight before the both of them.

"Lead on Spirit, the last time we met the night was waning fast and time was then precious, in this moment it is even more so. Lead on Spirit and I shall follow."

The ghost glides across the floor of the chamber raising both arms as it moves, all around plunges again into darkness the candle dies and the once roaring fire becomes embers before falling cold.

The city begins to spring up about them, Scrooge stares intently as the scene begins to grow and take form, the ghost points at a house on the opposite side of the street to where they now stand. Scrooge recognises it instantly as he had when he had visited the same property such a short time ago with the talkative large Ghost of Christmas Presents, its brashness and happiness in absolute contrast to the ghost in his presence at this time.

It was not Leadenhall Street and his immediate thought is that in this future also it seems Fred and Lily have remained in the old house. He sees people making their way through the street opposite them and passing right by where they stand, each and every one of them is wrapped up in a scarf or with gloves on or with their collars pulled up to protect them from the heavily falling snow that is being whipped up by a sudden fierce wind. He feels not a speck of cold or wind on his face although his nightcap moves to and fro with the weather.

"Spirit, what do you want me to do? Direct me and I shall obey" Scrooge says to the silent spectre behind him. The frightening hand of the ghost appears over Scrooges shoulder and points toward the front door of Fred and Lily Holywell.

"Do my Nephew and his lovely wife have children in this future Spirit?" Scrooge asks knowing that he will receive no reply from the ghost of Christmas Yet To Come, the bony hand of the spectre does not move and continues to point. "I will move on" Scrooge speaks although not a single person in the street hears him.

He steps from the pavement and crosses the deep snow on the roadway, not a horse or carriage has been through and it remains as virginal as when it fell from the sky, landing gently on other perfect flakes without sound or damage. Scrooge looks behind to where he expects to see the ghost pointing at Fred's home, the spectre has gone and despite a quick and frantic search around the immediate area it is nowhere to be seen.

"Spirit? Have you left me?" he calls out.

"Spare a coin for Christmas Sir?"

Scrooge jumps, he is startled and sees a thin girl sitting almost in the gutter of the street, she is dressed in rags and the shoes on her feet are so broken and cracked she may as well not be wearing any at all. Her complexion is grey and pallid, she looks hungry and is certainly suffering from coldness in her very bones. He crouches down next to her.

"Can you see and hear me?" he asks with hope in his voice. "I have no money with me at this time but with the spirits guidance I will return as soon as I can to help you, of course I will"

"Get out of the way!" A gruff unpleasant voice shouts.

Scrooge realises quickly that the girl cannot see or hear him, it was not he whom she was begging to for help but to the gentleman approaching her, he ignores her pleas and her outstretched arms. He pokes her with his walking cane as he passes, Scrooge stands up with a look of confusion on his face as the man in the expensive great coat, stockings and long boots walks on.

"Jacob?" he says. "Jacob Marley!" he shouts at the man who has walked past the desperate child as he is certain it is his long dead, or a man he though long dead, former partner in business. The man walks on without looking back at either the girl or the angry figure of Ebenezer Scrooge. The child stands up and wipes her face on her tattered dress, the tears cleaning dirt from just a tiny area on her cheeks, Scrooge helplessly puts his hands out toward the girl as she begins to walk away, her feet dragging through the ever deepening snow.

The door to the house opens and Fred appears and looks up and down the street, a street that is suddenly quieter than it was just a few minutes earlier. The snow is falling with such ferocity that the image of the child disappears from Scrooges view in a short instant, he hears Fred shout back into the house.

"Not a soul to be seen my dear, it must have been the wind bashing the old door knocker!" He sounds as happy as he always has, his infectious personality in full view even though there is not one single person around to benefit from it. As he begins to close the door to step back into the warmth inside, Scrooge nips past him into the hallway.

"Bless you child, if I can help you then I will" Scrooge says without begin heard. He suddenly stands up straight and puts both hands to his face, he believes in this very instant that he recognised the girl, a girl who is older than the ragged person Scrooge had just seen in the street. The person he believes it to be has seemingly been ravaged by poverty, hunger and sickness. "Belinda Cratchit, was that you?" he asks aloud and looks around the hallway. Fred has moved into the living room and he is standing alone in the dark, he can see light escaping from around the door and music from a piano being played on the other side. "Belinda Cratchit?" he says once more as he moves through the door.

Scrooge sees the darkness of the spectre standing in the far corner of the living room, it is unseen and unheard by the Holywell family.

"Now then children" Fred claps his hands as Lily finishes playing a Christmas carol. "Gather round for the festive hanging of your stockings!"

The three children all cheer with glee and run from the piano to the fireplace.

"Me first please Papa!" the youngest child jumps into Fred's lap.

"Young Frances, you are so full of life and excitement!" Fred gathers her up and holds her firmly in his arms. He becomes very serious, Frances and the other children settle down immediately as he clears his throat. "I need to be certain that you have been very good this year" he looks at Frances who's face breaks into a huge smile.

"You know I have Papa! I told you so only this morning!"

Fred looks at the other two children, both of whom are desperately trying not to giggle as their little sister pleads her case to her father.

"Very well, now if you can whisper in my ear what you would like Father Christmas to bring you?"

Frances leans forwards and puts her hand over Fred's ear and in a huge whisper, so loud that all in the room heard it, she says.

"A dolly please"

The two young boys begin to laugh but stop when Fred looks them sternly.

"Silence please Samuel and Noah, this young lady is telling me and me alone her very secret Christmas gift wish" he winks playful at his sons as Lily puts her hand to her mouth to stifle a giggle. "Are you sure Frances, because once you have made your wish to me then it cannot be changed"

Frances nods solemnly and stands up next to the fireplace, she reaches up holding her stocking but is just too short to hang it.

"Papa, can you help me please?" she asks and looks at Fred with hope in her eyes, he scoops her up in his arms.

"Of course" he takes the stocking from her and they both hang it to the nail affixed to the wooden mantle above the fire.

"Now it is time for bed Fan" Lily stands next to her husband with her arms outstretched.

"But Mama, could I just stay to hear what the boys ask Father Christmas for?" the young girl asks.

"Certainly not" Lily speaks with a serious tone. "I shall take you to your bed and the boys will follow in just an instant"

Frances is transferred from one parent to another after kissing her Father on the cheek.

"I just won't sleep a wink!" Frances speaks as Lily, who has a freshly lit candle in a silver holder in her hand, takes her from the living room and to her room.

"Now boys, who is next!" Fred asks Noah and Samuel, both shout 'Me!' at the same time.

Scrooge watches on as the boys repeat the same procedure as their younger sister, whispering their wish into Fred ear before they both shake his hand and bid him a good night.

"Straight to bed and to sleep now boys!" he tells them as they both leave the room.

Fred takes a small parcel from inside his jacket and ties it to the tree with a smile on his face, he stands back and admires the festive scene that surrounds him, the candles upon the mantle are near to their end and he takes two fresh from the drawer beside his chair.

"Let us not light any more Fred, we have the fire glow to keep us company" Lily has entered the room and is gently closing the door.

"Is Frances going to be awake and full of vigour all night my love?" he asks his wife.

"Not at all" she replies. "She was asleep within seconds of being tucked in tightly under the blankets!"

Fred stands up as his wife sits in the chair opposite his.

"Shall we have a sherry?" he asks.

"Yes please, that would be very welcoming Fred"

"I made my usual visit to see Uncle Ebenezer this morning"

Lily accepts the small glass of sherry her husband has poured for her.

"How was he?"

Fred smiles.

"As he usually is, he is such a comical fellow and that is the truth, he is as pleasant as he always is and I have nothing at all to say against him!"

"Will he come to dinner tomorrow do you think Fred, to see the children?"

Fred smiles but it has sadness throughout it.

"I fear not, I asked him of course and yet again thanked him for his generosity toward us"

"Fred Holywell, you have never taken one copper coin from your Uncle and he has offered many times!" Lily sips at her sherry. "He has made Scrooge and Wilkens what it is today, a successful business run by a very successful man"

"He does love the children so Lily and he is very fond of you as we know so well" Fred looks into his small glass and swills the contents without tasting them. "I have always loved Uncle Ebenezer" he looks at his wife with tears forming in his eyes. "Despite what happened to Mother and how he blames himself for it all"

"Tish Fred Holywell!" Lily's outburst surprises Fred who gasps with just a tiny intake of air, "If he wants to feel bad all year round because he blames himself for something he had not an inkling of, then so be it! He feels he let your mother die Fred and that is not fair on himself or on you"

"Lily please" Fred speaks quietly as he stares into the fire as it flickers and spits. "He knows he wants, even needs business more than family and when Mother truly needed him he was not there"

"Fred, please do not put yourself through this again"

"My love, it hurts my soul to think that the old man will forever blame himself for what Mother did. An ungodly act I think we can all agree but she did it never the less"

"Your mother never did get over the death of your father and that kind of hurt can never be fixed by any physician let alone Ebenezer Scrooge. All the money in the world could not have stopped her"

Fred reaches across and takes his wife by the hand.

"Thank you Lily, thank you for your counsel, as always you bring truth and light to everything in this family"

They sit in silence for several minutes, both listen to the howling wind at the window and to the crackle of the wood in the fireplace as it burns away.

"He may turn up for dinner Fred, stranger things have happened I am sure"

"It is such a shame that Dick Wilkens died before the business really took off after old Fezziwig left it to them both. Now Uncle Ebenezer runs it on his own and it is how he wants it to be. I fear he is lonely and it saddens my heart, especially at Christmas"

"He will be just as he wants to be, he is not unpleasant in any way but I do agree, I feel he is very lonely indeed"

"We have our children Lily and we shall never be lonely in this house" he says to her.

"And we have each other Fred, we shall always have each other" Lily squeezes his hand as she speaks.

"Merry Christmas" Fred says as he leans across the front of the fire and kisses his wife gently on the lips.

"Spirit" Scrooge sounds panicked as the Hollywell's living room fades into darkness. "My sister Fan, she is dead?" he asks before adding. "Again"

The ghost rises up in the dim light and points toward a set of iron gates, beyond them lies a churchyard covered in snow, all the graves are as silent as they should be. Scrooge looks on and sees three ladies standing around one gravestone just inside the gates.

"I should wait until their visit and mourning are complete Spirit. It would seem coarse of me to walk in at this moment of grief"

The ghost does not move, the hand points toward the gates of the churchyard without wavering. Scrooge nods and steps off alone leaving the ghastly form of the spectre outside of the consecrated grounds.

The churchyard is cold and grey in the dim light, dark snow filled clouds above threaten to unload at any moment, adding to the inches already lying on the frozen ground.

"This is a worthy place" Scrooge whispers as he enters through the iron gates and stands amongst the gravestones and the dead, he can hear the three women talking.

"So many years have passed" the oldest of the group speaks firmly as she places a small bouquet of flowers onto the grave in front of the stone marking the final resting place of the departed soul.

Scrooge, who recognises the speaker is suddenly aware of a chill behind him, he turns and the ghost stands in the gateway, silent and unmoved by its surroundings.

"Spirit, I said it before and I must say it again to you so please forgive the repetition" he moves away from the three women and stands in front of the ghost. "Before I draw nearer to this stone that is protected by these ladies, answer me one question, the same question that remained unanswered on your previous visit and remains unanswered to this very day" Scrooge takes a look around as snow begins to fall. "Are these the shadows of things that will be or are they shadows of things that may be only?"

The hooded figure remains as still as the graves that litter the churchyard, lifting its arm slowly it points toward the three women, one is very elderly and stands with the aid of an ancient crooked stick, the other two are younger but both are headed toward the end of middle age.

"I understand Spirit, I will move toward them in a moment, but can you tell me, can this be the final word in my life? Can the ends be changed yet again or is this it? What can you show me that I can understand?"

As has always been with the ghost of Christmas Yet To Come, no words are forthcoming to Scrooge, the pointing hand is the only constant in this moment.

"I know these women Spirit. Mrs. Fezziwig who seems sprightly despite her great age and I believe that to be two of her daughters with her"

The spirit moves its pointing claw toward Scrooge and then back to the gathering of grieving women.

"I understand" Ebenezer says and he moves toward the gravestone without speaking anymore to the silent ghost who does not follow him.

Scrooge looks down at the stone and reads the name upon it, he throws his head back and howls as if he were a beast from the wilds.

"No!" he cries. "No!"

Not one of the three ladies present reacts to him as he stares at the gravestone.

Here lies the body of

ISABEL SCROOGE nee Fezziwig

Farewell.

Born February 1st 1786

Died January 2nd 1810

"Mother, how we miss our Isabel" one of the daughters speaks to her sister and mother.

"We must not forget others on this day" Mrs. Fezziwig tells her daughters. "Many a death goes unmarked hereabouts but we shall never forget our Belle"

All three bow their heads in silence as Scrooge looks on, he glances at the ghost who has lowered his hand and stands in its own darkness at the gates.

"How can he live with himself Mother? How can that man that married our Belle live with himself!" the youngest of the trio cries out, she is comforted by her mother with a firm grip on her arm.

"Mary, you must not cast him a thought, you have your own family to think of, remember we are here for Belle and not for him" Mrs. Fezziwig wipes the covering of snow from the top of the slightly curved gravestone. "He left her without means, without children to occupy her mind and to calm her thoughts, his world is that of business, a business left to him in goodwill and faith! He may be prosperous in business but I hope his soul is filled with grim darkness"

"Mother, please do not upset yourself, we should celebrate the lives of those passed and not give a thought to those that survive them" Annie speaks with firmness to her mother.

Mrs. Fezziwig looks at the gravestone next to her dead daughters final resting place, the grave of Nigel Fezziwig.

"I am sorry for my words Husband, none of this is of your doing, you would not have left her almost penniless as he did, although she never asked him for a single coin to survive upon!" she lets out a sob but rebuffs both her daughters who step forward to aide her. "I am fine ladies, honestly and from deep in my heart I am fine but I too have darkness in my soul because of what he made her do"

The three women hold hands in a circle and stand in silence as the snow becomes heavier with flakes as large as fists landing on their bonnets and outer coats in a gentle manner befitting of the scene.

Scrooge has no words, he has a pain in his throat that is in need of escaping in the form of a noise that would be so unworldly that it may very well awaken those long dead in this churchyard. He turns to the gates to address the ghost.

It is gone.

"Spirit?" he calls out and steps back to walk out from the churchyard. "Where are you at? Have you left me alone yet again?"

Mrs. Fezziwig and her two daughters walk past him, he is unseen by any of them, he watches as they are met by two gentlemen, the husbands of Annie and Mary he presumes, they both lift their top hats a little and both offer their arms to Mrs. Fezziwig who stands in between them and accepts both offers of support. They move off and out of sight, disappearing into the snowstorm, Scrooge listens until he can hear them no more, he is glad that he does not hear his name mentioned again by any of them.

"Spirit" he calls out again as the clouds become just a little darker and the snow falls just a little heavier than it has been. Movement catches his eye in the church porch, it has no outer door and this leaves its innards open to the elements and snow has built up against the large wooden door to the church itself. The gable roof with its slates covered in a purest white that stands out in the darkness of this time and against the grey stone of the church, a simple unadorned wooden cross stands clean and without snow on it at the very front peak of the roof.

He sees the movement again in the shadows of the porch and he calls out again to the ghost but receiving no answer as has become expected. Scrooge walks up the pathway toward the church passing by an ancient Yew tree with a gnarled and twisted trunk that rises upward and away from the moss covered gravestones and tombs that surround it. As he passes underneath the epic canopy of the age old tree he glances at a gravestone that stands directly by the pathway, a stone with an ornate carving of an angel at its top, it has clear writing on it albeit it partially covered in snow that has been blown onto it, freshly laid flowers adorn its base. Scrooge stops and looks to read the words upon it. He is struck paralysed, unable to move, his eyes fixed on the name that burns into his heart causing it to cry out as if in immense pain.

"It cannot be" he whispers without moving. "This confirms my greatest fears, this confirms the words of my Nephew" his voice is hoarse as he speaks. "Little Fan is dead"

The words on the stone stand out in the dimness of the tree canopy and the ever darkening clouds above.

In Memory of

FRANCES 'FAN' HOLYWELL nee Scrooge

Mother, Wife and Sister. Missed every day.

Born April 28th 1790

Died Decemb

Scrooge is unable to move to wipe away the snow that covers the date of his dear sisters death, tears run down his wrinkled cheeks freely, he makes not a single attempt to stop them.

"Fan died anyway, after all this turmoil?" he shouts as he looks up, "When did she die Spirit? Can you tell me and release me from this moment of misery?"

He looks up and sees the ghost of Christmas Yet To Come standing in front of the huge trunk of the ancient Yew, it looks not out of place amongst the tombstones and beside the tree. His temporary paralysis gone he moves toward the snow covered tombstone, he is keen to uncover the date, keen to know when his sister passed away, keen to settle the screams that currently live inside his head seemingly unable to escape.

"I must know!" he says as he reaches forward with his hand.

A huge tumultuous wind takes him by surprise, it makes his nightcap move as if it were a flag atop a castle battlement, his dressing gown is nearly blown apart as the cord begins to untie as the wind pushes harder and harder into his body. He abandons his attempt to wipe the snow away from the gravestone as he grabs either side of his dressing gown and pulls it quickly together again although he cannot feel the coldness from it, he can feel the force it blows with.

The ghost of Christmas Yet To Come has both arms raised and Scrooge can see the thinnest of flesh barely clinging to them, the darkness begins to take the surrounding scenery away from Scrooge, it closes in on him and onto the gravestone of Fan. He lunges forward toward it to wipe the snow away, to see the date of her death, he needs to know his decision to change has not been for the worse, he must know that his decision for her to survive has not been in vain.

His face hits the ground as Fans final resting place disappears from view, in front of his very eyes everything changes and he finds himself lying in the snow, he looks up from his lowly position and sees the spectre standing behind another gravestone. He has a moment of joy, which is odd in his current circumstances but the joy is that he will find out the date he yearns so much, it is not to be. Scrooge stands up and looks at the ghost who has adopted the familiar pose of pointing, his horrible hand aimed at the stone in front of Scrooge, as he looks he has sudden realisation that this is not the headstone of Fan Scrooge. This has no angel adorning it nor does it have neat ornate writing, it is very plain and very simple. Some might say it was the marker of a pauper.

Here Lies

TIMOTHY CRATCHIT

Died 31 December 1843

The blandness and simplicity of the roughly carved headstone is not lost on Scrooge, he looks at the ghost who raises his arms again and before Ebenezer can say anything the darkness envelopes everything around him once again.

As the world begins to re take form around Scrooge, he takes a moment to digest what he had seen for just that fleeting moment. Tim Cratchit is dead, that is what he now knows for certain in this future, Tiny Tim Cratchit is dead and has been so for nearly ten years.

The ghost is pointing at a sign, a smart looking sign outside of a building that Scrooge knows only too well, it is the building that is his place of work, the counting house where he worked with Jacob Marley in a previous time and now with his Senior Clerk Bob Cratchit and his apprentice, Tim Cratchit.

"He cannot be dead, he is my apprentice clerk" Scrooge grumbles with sadness as his eyes follow the direction of the ghosts hand. The sign is green with firm, bold black lettering on it.

JACOB MARLEY

Since 1804

"Jacob?" Scrooge has his eyes screwed up so he can focus on the sign. "Not Scrooge and Marley?"

The Spectre has not moved, it points to the sign without any indication that his position will waver and Scrooges questions can be answered.

"No Scrooge and Marley in this future? This cannot be, Jacob and I were men of business. I understand now and have done for this past decade that not all of our business was decent toward my fellow man but it was business" he looks at the ghost. "I learnt that lesson last time Spirt, changes have been made in my life, changes for good"

The ghost does not move, Scrooge stares into the abyss of the blackness that is the inside of the very deep hood in an attempt to see a flicker of life, to see a glint of an eye but it is all but impossible to detach what he sees from the darkness of night.

"You wish me to go inside Spirit? To see this future after my changes have been made" he hangs his head. "Changes that seemingly prolonged the life of my sister but for how long I do not know and believe I will never know"

Ebenezer Scrooge moves forward toward the door to the counting house, a door he knows so well as he has entered through more times than there are days in a lifetime, he can hear raised voices from inside.

"Get out and be thankful I am not calling the constable or the night watchman!"

Scrooge recognises the voice instantly, it is Jacob Marley who is shouting, he steps back as the door opens suddenly. "Get out thief!"

Jacob Marley stands holding the open door in one hand and pointing into the street with the other. Scrooge recognises the great coat, stockings and long boots as those he had seen earlier outside of Fred and Lily's house, this confirms that the gruff man who stands just inside the counting house is his former partner and is the very same gruff man who treated the begging girl so badly, a girl whom Scrooge still believes to be Martha Cratchit.

"Jacob? What vexes thee so?" Scrooge asks but his question is unheard, another voice he recognises can be heard from inside. He takes two steps forward and sees Bob Cratchit standing inside the building, he has his old hat held in front of him and he is almost wringing it out with both hands.

"Sir, it was a very minor mistake, one that I can easily correct, I have certainly not stolen from you and nor would I" he sounds fragile and scared and stands stock still.

"Your mistake cost me one pound, ten shillings and sixpence Cratchit, you are not in a position to pay it back to me we both know that, so in my books that makes you a thief and a bad debtor"

"Sir, please, I am neither of those" Bob pleads with Marley. "I have never stolen a single penny from you and nor will I ever!"

"At least we agree with that Mr. Cratchit" Marley said and this seemed to calm Bobs shattered nerves.

"Thank you Sir" he replies with a huge sigh.

Marley looks at his clerk with a face resembling thunder.

"What I mean Mr. Cratchit is that you will be unable to steal from me because you Sir are without position"

"But Sir..." the desperate clerk begins to speak.

"No Sir!" Marley's voice booms into the street. "My business has gone from strength to strength and that is due to my singlemindedness and being without fear when decisions are to be made"

"My family Mr. Marley, what of them?" Bob is nearly on his knees pleading with his now former employer.

"What of them?" Marley asks without the least concern in his voice. "I shall see to it that you are known as a thief and a bad debtor, your family should they wish to remain with you should suffer the same indignity you shall!"

In an unusual pique of anger, Bob Cratchit turns on Marley.

"I have worked for you for many years, ignoring the terrible cost to the poor and those who borrow money from you, their suffering is of your doing Mr. Marley, yours and yours alone!"

Jacob Marley laughs, it is a sound not made by an angels tongue but more the rasp of an old dog nearing the end of its days.

"Well it seems that Bob Cratchit has more moral fibre than I gave him credit for!"

Bob has returned to wringing his hat in between his hands and staring at the plain tiled floor of the office.

"Sorry Sir, I was not quite myself for a moment"

"You were not Sir"

"It is Christmas eve Mr. Marley." Bob says quietly.

"Then you shall have plenty of time to return any gifts you have purchased and then you may be able to get some monies refunded. I care not for Christmas and I care not how you spend yours"

Bob Cratchit realises that his situation is hopeless, he puts on his scarf and hat and steps out of the counting house, he stands next to Scrooge without seeing him.

"If my position is no longer Mr. Marley, may I please take my wages owed"

Jacob Marley stares at his former clerk.

"Wages? Wages? What on this earth do you mean? You owe me the sum of one pound ten shillings and sixpence Mr. Cratchit! I shall take your wages in lieu of payment toward this debt, be thankful I am of a mind only to take the fifteen shillings you earn as cost toward your mistake!"

"Please Sir" Bob says as the door to the counting house is slammed in his face. "What do I tell Emily and the children?" he speaks aloud but not one person hears his words.

Scrooge watches as Bob slowly moves through the snow covered cobbles, his shoulders slumped and his head down, he is a broken man.

Without seeing the Ghost of Christmas Yet To Come, Scrooge knows the spectre has raised both his arms as the vision of Bob walking away from him disappears into blackness.

The kitchen of the Cratchit household at Camden Town is cold, as it realises in front of him Scrooge can see frosted breath coming from each of the mouths of the four people sitting around the dirty table, the fire is unlit and the windows grimy. Scrooge can just about see through them to a damp and frosty day outside, he can see blurred twinkling coloured lights from the festive lanterns illuminated in houses nearby.

"Spirit, is this the same Christmas or is this a different future?" he asks without expecting a reply.

The ghost points at the corner of the room by the cold fireplace. There stands a crutch, the sort of crutch a child would use, Scrooge takes a sharp intake of breath and puts his hand over his heart. Sadness overwhelms him.

"That crutch is covered in cobwebs and dust as if it has been there for many years. Spirit how far in the future are we now?"

Ebenezer stops talking as Emily Cratchit who has been sitting with her head in her hands addresses her children, he finds it difficult to ascertain their ages as they are all dirty, thin and dressed almost in rags. He recognises Belinda as the girl who was begging outside of Fred's house.

"We lose the house before the new year" Emily speaks slowly and with despair and desperation in her tone. "Mr. Marley has foreclosed and he takes possession without delay"

Martha looks up at her mother, she is pale, thin and dishevelled.

"Where do we go Mother?" she asks. "Are we destined for the work house or worse to prison?"

Emily looks at her children and a tired smile appears on her face.

"It is possible, we may of course find work and our luck will change but since your Father disappeared and it became known that he was a thief and could not pay his debts it becomes more difficult by the day to shake the reputation"

"Father is not a thief!" Peter Cratchit explodes. "That old miser Marley spread untruths to all who will listen, Father never stole a penny from him and his words have caused us to lose everything"

"Why did he go out and never return?" Belinda asks them all.

"We shall probably never know, but I fear the worst for him" Emily answers.

"I would like to wring the neck of that old misery Jacob Marley!" Peter stands up and the chair falls to the ground with a loud clatter.

Ebenezer Scrooge turns to face the ghost, it is a relief for him to avert his eyes from the scene of abject poverty and the destruction of a family he has grown to think of as his own.

"I see empty chairs by the fireplace and a family suffering" Scrooge says thoughtfully, he looks up at the ghost who stares back at him without eyes that can be seen. "Chairs! The Ghost of Christmas Presents said chairs, not chair but chairs as in more than one"

Scrooge staggers as the reality of this awful situation takes grasp of him, he holds onto the wall to stop himself falling onto the dusty stone floor of the kitchen.

"There should be a pudding singing in the tub, a festive tree lit in the corner, the fire should be warming the very souls of this family and most of all, Tim and Bob should be here with their family"

Scrooges realisation of this future, this bleak scene in front of him is more than he can bear without knowing the date of the Christmas eve in front of him or the truth of what happened to Bob and Tim Cratchit. He feels empty and at this very moment he believes his whole life has been worthless. All the changes he made and hoped were for the better are all gone in an instant.

"I cannot bear it Spirit" he whispers as the pain in his chest becomes more and more real.

With arms raised the ghost takes itself and Ebenezer Scrooge from this time that is causing the old man such pain in his heart and mind.

The church of St. Michaels in the city blossoms into view, Scrooge stands in the churchyard next to the silent ghost, he sees a notice outside of the church and moves across to read it, he looks back at the hooded figure who has remained in place.

"Spirit, this notice is for the funeral of Jacob Marley, it says here that the year is 1884" he counts on his fingers before speaking again. "Old Marley was ninety nine years old when he died, what a great feat to live to such an age!"

Scrooges momentary outburst is cut short as he sees the ghost pointing to a group of men standing outside of the grand church. He moves closer so as to be able to hear their words spoken to each other, he does not know any of the men from his time in business.

"He died a very rich man if all is to be believed" one says to the group, they all laugh.

"Richer than all of us together I should say!" another answers.

"Money never made him a decent sort though did it?" a young man in the group chirps happily. "Let us all be truthful as we are standing in this place of religion and sanctity, Jacob Marley was a mean, despicable and despised character!"

"Bravo to that, well said!" the eldest member of the group shouts gleefully, they all giggle as a man of the cloth stares at them intently as he is unhappy with their jollity at this supposed sombre occasion.

"Time for us to take our leave gentlemen" the young man says. "Time for us to move on and to forget about Jacob Marley and the misery he caused both the rich and the poor. I for one will not miss him one tiny piece!"

The group walk away from the church and Scrooge moves back to the spirit.

"I shall not ask to seek words of comfort about this man and his death" he wipes tears from his eyes. "Does this situation remind you of anyone else spirit?" he asks as the church of St. Michael disappears into shadows that become darkness leaving Ebenezer Scrooge alone with the Ghost of Christmas Yet To Come.

"Where are we Spirit?" Scrooge is downhearted, his time with the ghosts has not been as fulfilling and as joyous as he had wanted. "I am in a bind , the anguish and mental torture is just too much to bear at times, I have to admit that old feelings of rage, old feelings of hatred are rising within me. I have to admit that I do not like these feelings, nor do I wish to keep them" he takes a deep breath as the ghost raises its arms again. "No more Spirit, please no more! I have seen enough of the future to last me more than a dozen lifetimes, spare me seeing any more!"

They are soon standing among the graves of an old churchyard, the hooded figure points down to one, just as he had ten years previously. Scrooge had been frightened then, he remembers trembling and almost begging the dark spectre to tell him that this was not so, that these things could be changed. Shadows from the past, the presents and the futures he has seen cross his mind as he closes his eyes and clasps his hands in front of his body.

"I know this is a tombstone you wish me to see, I asked you before and I shall ask you again. Are these the shadows of the things that will be or are they shadows of things that may be? Tell me Spirit, change happened before and it was good, my choices then were decent and sound" he hangs his chin to his chest. "Maybe not so on this occasion"

He looks down at the stone the ghost is still pointing to, the Spirit is immovable as it ever was or has been.

"I will read it if you wish Spirit, but must we see sadness to learn that things should be left as they are?" he pauses and takes in a deep breath, he holds it before letting go in one huge exhale. "Did I do this for Fran, Fred or for me?"

The ghost lowers its outstretched arm, nothing else about it moves, it remains in self shadow and in mystery.

"I understand Spirit, consequences can be dire, even when changes are made seemingly for the better" he sighs heavily, kicks at the snowy ground then stands up straight as a guardsman and with great gusto calls out.

"Tell me it can change Spirit, tell me that Tim will live on and the Cratchits are all well and will all live to see many more festive and joyous Christmas eves!"

Ebenezer Scrooge turns his head away from the ghost in front of him, he wipes tears from both eyes, his sadness is not for himself but for everyone else, for those he has helped and for the one person he wants to help but knows in his heart that change is a dangerous and untamed animal. His voice becomes a tiny sound, almost as if he does not want to hear the words himself.

"Can it all go back Spirit? Although my heart breaks for my little sister Fan, my love for her remains as it always has and will do until the very last second of my life. In my last breath I will think of her"

The ghost begins to raise both arms but stops when Scrooge asks for just one more minute in this time, its arms slowly return by its sides.

"I am gladdened by your visit to me Spectre, glad I am not witnessing distain or even hatred toward me. For that I will be eternally grateful to you and to the other spirits who have visited me on this day and previously"

Scrooge points to the tombstone that the ghost had been pointing at when they had arrived in this space on earth, it is the only stone in view, all the others around have faded into the incoming darkness.

"I do not fear this as I did Spirit. I understand that it is thought that I may have been trying to save my own soul and heart, but that is not the case. Although the words of the ghost of Jacob Marley scared me, and if I am honest my fear of death has been constant in my life, I have become accepting of them, of what it means for me and for others. If I have learnt anything at all from my experience with the Spirits it is that it is quite possible that when this life as we know it is over then another may begin" he smiles at the unmoving hooded figure. "I find the not knowing quite calming and exhilarating at the same time"

He turns his back on the lone tombstone guarded by the Ghost of Christmas Yet To Come and pushes his hands deep into his dressing gown pockets.

"I have no need to see my tombstone Spirit, I know the dates by heart and I am satisfied"

The vision of the tombstone fades and is gone before Ebenezer Scrooge can turn back to face it.

"Sacrifice and decisions are always difficult" he says to the ghost. "I tried to make things better before they were already better in my lifetime. I suppose in some seeing eyes things were for the good, but not for mine. Let us not change what has been and learn from it, however heart breaking it may be"

He turns to face the ghost for the final time, getting onto his knees he pleads for all to change back to how it was, for him to be the miserable miser he was bringing misery as he did so, never to marry and for his only sister to die young. He begs for Fred and Lily to remain married and to be happy and for wealth not to destroy any part of their lives, he asks for Belle to live and to marry and to be happy for ever. Most of all he wants the Cratchits to be happy and to live comfortably, never to fall into debt, for Bob to be alive and with his family and most importantly to Ebenezer Scrooge, for Tim not to die.

The Phantom is suddenly exactly as it had been but somehow larger and Scrooge detected a new meaning in its solemn shape, just as he had ten years before, ten years ago this very night. With a wave of its bony hand the ghost bows its hooded head almost imperceptibly to Scrooge.

"Do I thank you Spirit or am I to suffer the change I made all in good heart?"

Scrooge holds up his hands as if in prayer wishing his fate, a fate he requested, be reversed. He spied a tiny alteration in the hood and gown of the Ghost of Christmas Yet To Come, it shrank, collapsed and dwindled into the shadows.

Stave V

The Last Carol at Christmas

Scrooge arrives back in his chamber and it is as if he has never left, the fire is burning nicely and the candle on the mantle is still living and flaming as though no time has passed at all. He looks at his old four poster bed and is glad to see that it is empty, he had feared another vision of a covered body lying upon it as before. He takes a few moments to look out of the window at a dark London Town, no tormented spirits can he see, it is just as it has been for many a year and just as it should be.

He takes off his dressing gown and hangs it neatly on the back of the chair facing the fire, his heart and soul are at peace with the world and most importantly, he is at peace with it all.

With a lightness in his step he moves to the bed and slips off his slippers, ensuring they are neatly next to one another underneath the frame. Climbing under the covers and pulling them up to his chest with his head resting firmly on the pristine white pillow of finest down, he crosses his arms comfortably on his chest.

"Merry Christmas dearest Fan" he whispers as he dies with a smile on his face.

"Where is he Robert? You don't think the old fool has ventured to Fred's instead of coming to us for Christmas dinner?"

Bob Cratchit laughs at his wife who is standing with her hands on her hips in the warm, clean and friendly kitchen.

"I think nothing of the sort my love, he is most likely behind on his time and there is still plenty to pass until he is actually late!"

"Go and get him if you please" Emily has returned sharply to the stove and is busying herself with pots and pans filled with oyster soup, potatoes awaiting boiling before mashing then to be mixed with boiled onions, carrots that have been finely chopped, turnips peeled and cabbages sliced.

"Oy! Oy!" a voice calls from outside the door. "Is it safe to enter?"

Emily and Bob look at one another and both smile knowingly.

"Come in if you want dinner!" Bob shouts and Emily laughs.

A man walks into the kitchen and closes the door quickly behind him.

"It's rasping cold out there!" he says as he rubs his hands together.

"Get to the fire Albert and warm through" Bob says to the visitor. "Our Belinda told that you were working all of the day today"

Albert Page rubs his hands vigorously and takes off his scarf and outer jacket to reveal that he is still dressed in state livery.

"A full complement is not needed today or tomorrow and we drew straws to see who could spend the days with family and I only won!"

Belinda appears at the kitchen door and in a manner not befitting any lady, she screams with happiness and runs to her husband throwing her arms around his neck.

"Albie!" she cries. "I am so happy to see you!"

"Easy now Belinda, we don't want...." he stops talking suddenly and looks at his wife then his in laws with wide eyes.

"It is alright Albie, I told all the family our news!"

Albert Page kisses his wife gently on the cheek.

"We are all so happy for you and our Belinda Albert" Bob shakes his son in laws hand vigorously.

"Thank you Sir" Albert replies.

"Enough of that!" Emily smiles as she scolds the men. "Bob, go and get the old miser and you Albert" she kisses him on the cheek and puts her arm around her youngest daughter.

"Go and drag Joseph from the dining room, he and Tim are entertaining David and Little Jane"

"What do you need with my husband?" Martha enters the kitchen and she and Albert hug affectionately. "Well done you!" she whispers in his ear causing him to blush just a bit.

"Thanks Martha" he replies before turning to Emily. "What am I to tell Joe you need us for Mother in Law?"

"To collect our enormous goose from the bakers at the market, I wanted to roast it here in front of the fire or in the oven but it is just too big, so the pair of you can fetch it if you please. By the time you return the potatoes will be boiled along with the rest of the vegetables. Tim can remain and look after the children"

"He will be pleased!" mutters Albert, just loud enough for Belinda to hear but quiet enough for Emily to miss it completely.

"And the pudding my love?" Bob enquires of Emily.

"In the pot Robert as well you know, you can go with your son in laws and collect old misery" she waves a spoon at the men. "Be off with you all, leave the women to finish this dinner and be warned gentlemen" she grins at them. "Do not stop at Simpsons Tavern for a glass or mug of anything!"

"Come my good fellows!" Bob is happy the day is going so well. "One goose and one old man to collect for dinner!"

With his scarf wrapped around his neck and his tall hat atop his head, he opens the door as Albert and Joe put on their outside coats, he kisses his wife on the top of her head and stands to attention at the door as the two other men leave the kitchen.

"A Merry Christmas Cratchits, Blakes and Pages!" Bob says with a flourish as he closes the door.

"I thank the Lord that my husband is a happy man but sometimes it is just too much!"

Belinda and Martha both giggle as they set about helping Emily and they listen to the fading sounds of the three men singing 'God bless you, merry gentlemen' in full voice.

Bob Cratchit leaves Joe and Albert as they cross toward Leadenhall Market and onto the bakers, a walk of less than a few minutes only, he continues on Lime Street toward the house of Ebenezer Scrooge.

The fog begins to fall and a pallid darkness is moving in to take the early afternoon brightness on this Christmas day. People are rushing about with many a 'Merry Christmas' on their lips to wish friends and strangers alike a fine day. The ancient tower of St. Michaels church with its gruff old bell that has cause to peep down and strike on the hour and the quarters with exactness and regularity, looms across the area across from the market where smoke and smells that delight rise into the air. Bob stands outside of Scrooges yard and inhales deeply imagining the last knockings of sales at the poulterers and greengrocers, where the poor will be waiting to buy some meat or vegetables for no more than a few pennies to celebrate a meagre Christmas day as they stand and sit patiently in their drab clothes that stand out amongst the brightness of the holly sprigs and berries.

"Delightful!" he says out loud, a lady and her child passing by look at him with curiosity, he raises his hat. "Merry Christmas to you both"

"And to you Sir" the lady replies as she hastens away.

Bob is left alone by the gated entrance to the courtyard of 45 Lime Street, a place he is familiar with and a place he enjoys visiting. The house is in darkness, even in this early part of the afternoon the current gloom should dictate that a candle or two should be lit within. He approaches the substantial front door and admires, as he always does, the old door knocker that all three of his children enjoyed pounding on the door when they visited Uncle Ebenezer when they were younger, the echoing of the 'rat a tat tat' inside the large hallway always made them cheer with joy.

'Rat a tat tat!'

Bob knocks upon the door and hears the familiar and comforting sound of the echo inside the building.

"Mr. Scrooge, it is I. Mrs. Cratchit sent me to assure her that you will not be late!" he has Christmas happiness in him that breaks through the gloom.

He steps back and looks up at the upper windows of the building, it is bearably dark in the courtyard due to the inclement weather that seems to be approaching and the distinct lack of gas lamps in this part of town.

"It is too early for lamps to be lit anyhow Bob Cratchit" he grumbles to himself as he steps back once again to see if he can glimpse a candle or fire lit within the old building.

Another solid use of the door knocker goes unanswered and Bob puts his hand on the round ornate brass knob and turns it slowly. It gives and moves in an anti-clockwise direction, he hears the latch turn and the substantial door opens, the deadbolt has not been engaged thus making entry very simple indeed.

"Mr. Scrooge?" Bob calls into the hallway only to be met with cold silence and a stillness that he finds eerie and unsettling. "Mr. Scrooge?" he tries again as he steps into the building. Before closing the door he takes a candle from the table inside of the door and lights it with matches from the small drawer at the front of the table, even in the brightest of summer days this windowless hallway is always a shadowy place, on this afternoon it is alive with emptiness and silence.

Bob moves onto the large staircase and carefully takes one tread at a time, calling out to the owner of the house at regular intervals, he reaches the top and stands impressively still outside of Mr. Scrooges chamber. No light emanates from under the door and not a sound is to be heard from behind it. Bob has been into this very room many times as his employer prefers to meet there to discuss any business or personal matters. Emily, Martha, Belinda and Tim have not ever, not even once set a single foot inside of it. When the family are invited to visit for any occasion then Mr. Scrooge always entertains them in the capacious living room on the ground floor, a room that Mrs. Dilber keeps in immaculate condition at all times, in contrast to the hallway it has large windows that allow light to drown its very interior.

As Bob opens the chamber door, it squeaks and squeals as if objecting to being pushed inward he calls out just once more.

"Mr. Scrooge are you in here Sir?"

He raises the candle into the gloom, the flickering flame causes shadows to dance from every wall and corner in the room, he sees the glow reflected in the only window of the chamber, the fire is cold and a fully melted candle lies finished on top of the mantle.

Then he sees him.

The cold in the room seems suddenly intense, he wishes the fire was alight and bringing life and colour into the room he now stands in.

Ebenezer Scrooge lies dead in his bed, his nightcap securely affixed to his head, his arms crossed demurely across his chest, he has the fixed smile of a dead man on his face.

Bob moves forward slowly and without fear. Sadness fills his heart as he stands next to the bed and looks down at his former employer.

He takes two pennies that he notes are placed on the bedside stand and gently puts one on each of the closed eyes of the cold body that lies before him as is the custom.

"Rest in peace Mr. Scrooge" he says quietly. "I hope you were able to move on as a happy man even though you were alone at that final time"

Bob moves away from the bed in respect for the life of the man that has died in it, he turns away and notices that a bowl lies smashed in the hearth and what appears to be dried soup has run down the old Dutch tiles that surround the fireplace.

Ebenezer Scrooges funeral is a big affair, St. Michaels Church, that has seen its fair share of events over the centuries, is packed to the rafters with those wishing to celebrate the life of their friend and colleague who had died suddenly on Christmas Day 1853. The cloisters, the north and south aisles have standing room only with each and every seat taken in the nave.

"A man that knew how to live" one rather jolly and corpulent fellow observes.

"A friend to the poor and a guide to the rich" said another.

"Generous to all and will be remembered as so" smiles a well-dressed lady seated near to the front of the church.

"A miser and a misery!" Emily Cratchit declares. "And I shall miss him and I thank him for our life"

The Cratchits are seated on the very front pew on one side of the church with Fred, Emily, Samuel, Noah and Frances seated on the other, young Fan is uncomfortable and wriggles on her seat until told to remain still and quiet by her mother.

"We shall not mourn the loss but celebrate the life of Uncle Ebenezer" Fred tells his family. He is happy that his only relative and the brother of his long departed mother had seen the light of life over ten years since, also that he and Fred had spent many a long hour together getting to know each other not only as kin and as men, but as friends.

Bob Cratchit feels a burning lump in his throat as he stands to read the eulogy, Fred had insisted it be him that must do the reading as his Uncle had become very fond of his clerk and all of his family. Scrooge had told Fred on more than at least a dozen occasions that he was always treated as a member of the Cratchit family when he visited them and for that he was ever grateful and more than a little ashamed of his past.

Bob stands facing the packed church that has settled quickly waiting for him to begin, he glances to the centre of the end of the nave in front of the sanctuary where the plain coffin with brass handles stands alone on a pair of oak coffin stands, the shiny brass plaque on the lid only has the name of Ebenezer Scrooge on it. Bob looks up at the impressive vaulted ceiling within the church, the polychrome plastered ceiling stands in contrast to the darkened wood support arches that are plain in their seventeenth century design. Suddenly a shaft of sunlight pushes through the gloom of the winters day outside and onto the large and frankly dull ancient stained glass window on the east wall of the church.

He takes a deep breath before he begins, he looks at Emily who smiles and nods at him encouragingly.

"He did it all, and infinitely more, he was a second father to my children and to the children of his nephew Fred" Bob looks across the church and Fred smiles at him. "He was as good a friend, as good a master, and as good a man as the old city knows, or any other good old city, town, or borough in the good old world." Bob is happy to hear slight murmurs of agreement and even some muffled laughter from the congregation. "And it was always said of him that he knew how to keep Christmas well, if any man alive possess such knowledge. May that be truly said of us and all of us! I finish the eulogy to Mr. Ebenezer Scrooge with a few good words said to him once when he most needed it." he pauses and looks up into the large gathering in front of him. "God bless us. Everyone"

Scrooge has been dead a few short months and winter clings onto London with the white blanket of snow refusing to leave as the New Year passes and then stayed for many weeks after the arrival of 1854.

Bob and Tim Cratchit are walking the short distance to the counting house from their home at Lime Street, keys jangle merrily in the pocket of Bobs long coat, keys to the building and the business he now proudly owns.

"Now then apprentice, when we get inside you must make up the fires and fill the coal scuttles before you dot a single i with your quill Tim Cratchit!"

"Yes Father" Tim replies before he quickly adds after a stern look from Bob. "Yes Mr. Cratchit!"

Bob takes the keys from his pocket and both men stand back and admire the new sign that hangs outside of the counting house. It proudly reads.

Scrooge, Marley and Cratchit

THE END

Printed in Great Britain
by Amazon

39561772R00089